Praise for the works of Matt Serafini

"Matt Serafini's deep kn[…]nre shines
in *Under the Blade*—a n[…] back glory
days, but spills new bl[…]nd style. I
loved it!"

– Brian Keene

"A great book."

– *Shock Waves* Podcast
on *Under the Blade*

"Matt Serafini is a literary writer with a heart full of slasher films. His stylish blood-soaked prose is a treat for all horror fans, intimidating to his cohorts, and a vehicle that brings the glorious violence and tension of 1980s horror screaming into the present."

– Gabino Iglesias, author of
Zero Saints and *Coyote Songs*

"Serafini makes bold decisions . . . horror fans and authors of this genre will surely applaud!"

–*Final Guys*

". . . takes you on one hell of a ride!"

– *Scream Magazine*

"Serafini displays a sure hand . . . a savage and blood-drenched read."

– *Horror After Dark*

"Serafini is energetic and entertaining, constantly keeping readers on their toes."

– *Wicked Horror*

Rites of Extinction

Matt Serafini

GRINDHOUSE PRESS

Grindhouse Press
PO BOX 521
Dayton, Ohio 45401

Grindhouse Press #050
ISBN-10: 1-941918-46-8
ISBN-13: 978-1-941918-46-3

Also by Matt Serafini

Novels

Ocean Grave

Island Red

Under the Blade

Devil's Row

Feral

Collections

All-Night Terror (with Adam Cesare)

1

REBECCA DANIELS IS SLUMPED INSIDE a rest stop booth. A plate of undercooked curly fries cools before her. Two paper cups, mustard and ketchup, sit in unmolested domes of yellow and red.

Everything's untouched.

The entering family has her full attention. The father, just a few years behind Rebecca, is fifty pounds overweight inside a loose Hawaiian shirt he thinks hides his gut. He carries a baby in a pink hat in one arm while using the other to hold his son's hand. The boy's eyes are like Christmas once he spots the golden arches. The way he begs for a Happy Meal is Pavlovian.

Mom strides in behind them, a pretty little trophy thing who looks like she's crawled on hands and knees from the pages of an Old Navy catalogue. The cell phone in the palm of her hand shows a GPS image and she points to the restrooms nestled in the far corner.

"We're making good time," she says. "So five minutes for the little boys' room and then we meet back here, okay?" She takes the baby girl in her arms and hurries off.

Dad watches her go and ruffles the top of his son's hair. Once mom's out of earshot he leans down and says, "Chicken nuggets?" The little boy takes his hand, starts dragging dad like a stubborn horse. "Let's go, Daddy. Let's go get chicken nuggets!" Dad laughs as they head toward the kiosk. They're about to pull one over on mom.

The ghost of a smile haunts Rebecca's otherwise sullen face. She remembers what these road trips used to be like. Touch and go, mostly. Chaotic in the moment, because it's all screaming kids, spilt milk, lost toys, and the exasperated discussions that happen around these crises. Last thing these vacations are is relaxing.

But memories have a way of crystalizing the happiness the further you get away from them.

Rebecca watches the dad lift his son up as they scrutinize the menu, openly strategizing the order. She can tell dad's got the stuff. That special ingredient that makes you one of the good ones. Anyone can become a parent. The physical act of doing so is nothing but biology. But that means jack without the rest.

You've got to want to do it.

Because nobody's impressed with your ability to have a kid. Most people on this earth have the tools necessary to plant a baby, watch it grow. It's more impressive to get a driver's license, gun permit, or college degree. You need to work for those things.

But a baby?

Nah.

Dad and son have landed on food. The dad steps back so the little boy can step to the counter and mumble his order. Rebecca doesn't hear the particulars from her vantage, only the atonal child's drone as he asks for "golden ketchup" and then explains it's for "my chicken nuggets." Everyone has a real cute laugh over this.

And, again, Rebecca knows she's right about daddy. One of those invested types. They're easy to spot because they go out in public without looking like they're dragging a human curse around with them.

Good parents are hard to find. An admittedly bleak worldview that stems from Rebecca's line of work, but she's got more than enough anecdotal evidence in her microcosm to justify it.

And hell, parenting is not easy. Whole years will pass before you know where you fall on the scale. But this dad . . . he's doing it right. Blood and tears.

Dad glances over, happens to lock eyes with Rebecca. She's jolted from her daydream and, now that she's been found out, reaches for a fry and throws an awkward wave with her free fingers.

He's quick to look away, searching out another spot for his eyes to nest before he turns back to the food. Rebecca nods to herself, thinking, yep, one of the good ones. Not only is he Father of the Year but mom's got his gaze on lockdown.

Mom reappears carrying the baby whose spring outfit doesn't look an inch out of place. Her footsteps echo on the permanently streaky rest stop tile.

"Steve," she says, "we're going to eat at my sister's."

Rebecca doesn't like her as much. Doesn't like this type at all. It's not as easy to tell where she falls on the scale. Stay-at-home mom, she guesses, which probably means she had to bury her own career in order to commit. Rebecca should be more sympathetic. Every parent makes sacrifices, some of them more severe than others.

As mom and baby rejoin the boys, mom laughs and smiles at the conversation, giving her husband a playful nudge of affection that may or may not be for Rebecca's benefit.

This family's got time. As much as any of them do. But it goes quick and the end is even harder on the good ones. It'll be brutal for them once the little ones are grown. Nobody warns you about Empty Nest Syndrome when you sign the parental contract, but it's a hell of a thing.

The family over there ain't thinking about it. But one day, Little Johnny and Little Julie are going to pack up the old ass Supra and drive off to four years of freedom, an academic layover before moving to some dirty-ass city because they think "all that culture" can cure the settling malaise inside of them.

When that happens, it'll be the parents who really suffer.

The cell phone on the table vibrates. The Formica surface grumbles, as if objecting to the message before she can read it. Rebecca doesn't have to read it to know the gist but flips it over and sighs.

Don't run, Becks.

The dad stares at Rebecca again. This is too much attention. She doesn't want to be remembered. But of course that's what's going to happen to a woman who can't keep her eyes to herself inside a rest stop.

Rebecca feels the need to go to them and foist her hackneyed advice. Words they would never hear, for they'd be too busy thinking about what a lunatic she is. So she stays where she is, thankful for the modicum of self-awareness she's still got.

But it's all true, goddammit, and they should know. Somebody should tell them. It's the parents who give their bodies and souls, only to be rewarded with feelings of worth and purpose. For a time.

Until they're left sitting in quiet living rooms like hollowed-out husks. And it's their fault because they've spent eighteen years as willing but indentured servants to their offspring and, really, the only kind of cold turkey anyone likes is Thanksgiving leftovers . . .

Another buzzing text:

Come home so we can sort everything out. Please.

This one barely registers. Rebecca's too busy watching the Family Of The Year. Not all parents are created equal. That's just the luck of the draw. Ask the deadbeat dad living under some bullshit assumed name in an Albuquerque walk-up if he's sad about never again seeing one of his daughter's dance recitals. Or the junkie mom who's thirty-two going on seventeen and leaves her eleven-month-old home alone in his crib six nights a week because he sleeps through the night and mom just needs, really needs, that chemical high in order to feel alive.

This family gets their greasy fast food bags and it's mom's turn to hold everything while dad takes the boy to "potty." They glide into earshot and Rebecca watches dad give mom a sly pat on the ass. "This way," he says, "he's guaranteed to eat and we'll enjoy Julie's company without having to worry every five seconds if he likes poached salmon or whatever the heck she's going to torture us with."

The boys of the family hurry off, leaving the mom to consider what a thoughtful man she's got. Probably already knows. She passes by without giving Rebecca a second look, but the infant throws a toothless grin over mommy's shoulder. A sight so sweet Rebecca can't help but mist at the sight of it.

All Rebecca has are memories from another life.

She was near the end. Empty Nest close enough to dread. She was finished with all the schedules and coordinating of softball practices, games, sleepovers, weekend excursions to the mall, and even college scouting.

What they don't tell you is that you know you've done it right if you think back on things and know in your heart it was worth it. That the part you played in creating life, in raising another human being under your own tutelage, was the most fulfilling thing you'll ever do. Because after you're gone and everyone forgets you even lived, only your children will know you existed at all.

It's the only way to live forever.

And if you're that deadbeat in Albuquerque or the junkie perma-teen, you'll never know that feeling. Yeah, you're a parent. But you're not a parent. And no one's gonna miss you when you're in the dirt.

Empty Nest is just another way of spelling circle of life. You're never really whole again, but you can sometimes fill that void with enough relics from your old life. Just enough to recover the scent. Just enough to remember the way you used to be.

Sometimes, though, Empty Nest happens before it should. Unnaturally. And that's a lot tougher to reconcile. When your child is taken from you, even those little fragments of your old life are out of reach. When your child is murdered, found in the heart of public conservation land, with a face slashed to ribbons and a heart stuck through, the grief swallows you whole.

There is no recovery.

The phone shakes again but Rebecca stuffs it into her pocket. The dad and son return from the restroom, the boy cheerfully mumbling something about how his hands aren't fully dry from that blowy thing, and Rebecca wipes another tear as she remembers how everything's a marvel at that age.

Life so full of wonder.

She wishes there was something left to surprise her.

The family regroups and leaves, the dad stealing one last glance at Rebecca. He smiles without eye contact and it's unclear what he means. Then they're gone, and Rebecca is alone with her fries. Doesn't remember why she ordered them in the first place. She hasn't eaten fried food in twenty years.

She tosses it in the nearest barrel and uses the bathroom, stopping just inside the doorway with hands curled around either side of the jamb. The row of mirrors cannot see her reflection from this vantage, and she steals a few quick breaths before she rushes past.

Whatever you do, don't look.

She reaches the anonymity of the far stall and locks the door, curious about the latest text. It says, *At least tell me where you're going.*

Beyond the stall, she hears the tapping. One finger *tinking* on glass.

Not now, she thinks. She's gotta find this place. Some 'burg she's never heard of. A town called Bright Fork.

Truth of it is, she doesn't even know how she knows that's where she needs to go.

It takes a few minutes to build up the courage needed to sprint past the glass again. No time to stop and wash her hands. She'll use the package of baby wipes she's got sitting on the passenger seat of her car.

Then she flings the stall door wide and sprints. The playful *tinks* hasten as her reflection blurs by, and then she's free of them. Rebecca hurries to the parking lot where frosted air irritates her lungs. She's underdressed because this spring is colder than most. A thin coat of frost entombs her car's dented body.

That's okay, though, because her insides are always on fire lately. Always too warm. A fever she can't seem to shake.

Every day on the road is like this now. All of yesterday, a dream. All of today, a nightmare.

2

REBECCA PULLS THE CAR OVER to the side of the road as soon as the headache hits. A trail of scorched rubber follows her taillights off the asphalt and into the dirty turnaround. The sign there reads: WELCOME TO BRIGHT FORK.

Normally, she'd soldier through this. Migraines are a hereditary ailment for Clan Daniels and she's never been a stranger to them. Got bottles of Advil in every room back home and two here in the car.

But this is more than just some migraine. It feels like spikes sliding behind her eyes. Pressure on her skull sends tears down her cheeks. She fumbles for the glove box as invisible hands squeeze her temples.

Her eyes feel ready to burst.

It's bad and getting worse.

The closer to Bright Fork she gets, everything's so much worse.

The liquid-filled capsules rattle around as she fishes the bottle out from beneath a pistol and a mess of crumpled owner's papers. She swallows four without water, a real pro at this, then sits for a moment massaging her skull while the worst of it passes.

Rebecca happens to glance out through the trees. Down into the valley cradling the town of Bright Fork in between a sweeping mountain range. A snow globe village, at this distance. She's much closer than she realized. To see it brings shivers. The sky above is etched in gray, making Bright Fork a raw and unwelcoming place.

The invisible vice begins to loosen around her head as the Advil kicks in. Rebecca manages to get upright, closes her hands around the steering wheel.

Let's get this over with, she thinks and starts on.

3

FIRST PLACE SHE STOPS IS the diner. Hubs of information when you're hunting the drifter class. Not everyone's got the scratch for a motel room, but almost anyone can scrounge a few quarters for coffee and pie.

Rebecca sits on the stool nearest the register, feeling like an old man on the beach with a metal detector. She thinks of these places as grain sifters. Every so often you shake your pan around until the sand falls through and only that lost Rolex remains.

Her Rolex is a man.

A killer.

She orders a vanilla Coke and a cheeseburger and the asshole working the grill makes a comment about how nice it is to see a good-looking girl with an appetite. She twists her mouth into a lopsided smirk that disappears before it has a chance to register as encouragement.

Just her way of ensuring he fucks off.

Cooks are never any help. Their workdays are sweat and sizzle and, in dives like this, sucking down Marlboro Reds out behind the dumpster whenever there's a lull. No. Thanks. It's waitresses who've got the answers. They know all the faces. And the stories that go with them.

That's what she needs today.

Rebecca needs one particular face.

She puts the photograph face up on the table as the woman brings her soda. Rebecca asks if she's seen him. The waitress picks up the photo and waves it between her fingers as she thinks it through.

The young man in the picture wears an Ivy League haircut, pomaded hair pushed away from the part.

Nope. The waitress ain't seen him, suggests maybe trying the Harvest Hill Motor Inn down the road.

Rebecca smiles warmly, slides the photo back into her pocket and presses the plastic straw to her lips, spelunking for syrup. "Thanks," she says, beginning to ascend on an afternoon sugar high. Sugar's poison, but she thinks she could get used to this.

The sweetness on her tongue riles old Thursday night memories. Dinner at the truck stop on Route 117, because Jaime thought their burgers were the best in the state. The only time she'd stop pouring vanilla soda down her throat was to take a big bite of one.

Rebecca never found the food there to be anything special, certain their salads came from a bag, and Jaime waved the accusation away. "Who orders salad at a truck stop, Mom?"

Rebecca's stomach turns as the waitress slides the burger in front of her. The smell of grease is enough to make her feel ill and, like the fries at this morning's rest stop, she wonders just what in the hell she's thinking.

Sorry, Jaime, she thinks and pushes it back. The waitress stares like her honor's been insulted.

"My fault," Rebecca says. "I'm not feeling well."

"I gotta charge you for it."

"Of course," Rebecca says. "Think I'll go see about that motel." She was going to try it anyway. Needs a place to stay, after all.

Sometimes, diners are no help.

4

BRET ANSWERS ON THE FIRST ring.

"Becks–"

"Stop it," Rebecca says. "And listen to me. I had one last night."

"One what?"

"A dream. Memory. I don't know . . . whatever you want to call it."

"That's two different things. Apples and shit."

"I have some questions."

"So do I."

"Mine are more important," she says.

"This wouldn't happen if you'd take your–"

"Meds? Fuck you. Pills make me forget."

"Meds help you to think straight."

"I don't want to do this every time we talk. I can't."

A long pause follows. Rebecca doesn't dare fill the silence because it's not hers to take. That's the agreement. Therapy was fuck all, except the first rule they happened to pull from it. This one. It wound up being useful.

Listen before speaking.

"Okay," Bret says. A defeated sigh that's still happy to be in communication. "Let's hear it."

"Remember that night on the beach?"

"Lots of nights on the beach."

"This was summer after senior year."

"I remember we spent time on the beach, sure."

"We were there with Sara and Ty. The more we drank, the naughtier things got? We wanted to screw in public and figured . . . the beach at night is public enough. Kept waiting for them to leave, but they wouldn't."

Bret says, "No."

"Come on."

"Never happened."

"Oh, god, will you stop doing this?"

"Becks . . . who the hell are Sara and Ty?"

"I," she starts, because at first the answer is obvious. Sara and Ty. Old friends. Rebecca's head is packed with memories of them. And at exactly the same time, she recognizes that Bret's right. It kills her to admit that, but she's never met these people.

They're faces in a dream.

"I can tell by the confusion in your voice that you don't know them any more than I do." His voice wears insufferable validation.

"I'm not crazy."

"If you have to say it—"

"Oh, fuck you."

"I'll just add this call to the list, then."

"Keeping score?"

"Keeping a log. Doctor said I should."

"Doctor." The word makes her spit. "There's nothing wrong with me."

"The house is so empty," Bret says. It's his way of pleading with her to get help. "Each time the furnace comes on, I think someone's in here with me. I pretend it's you, you know. Makes me remember the noises the house used to make when you'd get home late from work."

Rebecca closes her eyes. It's tempting to let him finish that story.

There's no time for comfort, though. No promises of better days coming back. "I need to go—"

"Get rip roaring drunk?"

"It's the only way to stop the confusion."

"Is it really?"

"Yes," she says. It only slows things down, and she'll take that. She'll take whatever she can get.

"Come on," he says. "Just because you think it's the only way doesn't make it so."

"I'm going."

"Where?"

"Just pulled into a motel." She hangs up without telling him about the mirrors.

5

"YOU FIND THIS PIECE OF shit, you tell him he owes me for three nights." The manager's name is Brian or Ryan or something equally utilitarian. She forgets as soon as he says it and it doesn't matter enough to ask for a refresher.

Rebecca says, "You've seen him, then."

The guy behind the counter has more than just seen him. You don't react this way when you've *seen* someone. The sight of Paul giving a smartass-y okay gesture with his fingers is enough to make this guy pop. His cheeks flare bright red like he's gotten into the Maybelline.

It's understandable. Paul leaves scars. That's what he does. And this guy's wearing more than a few. Rebecca is picking a few of his scabs clean.

"Are you listening to me?" he barks. "In forty years I've never rented to a kid–"

"Twenty-two is hardly a kid."

"Oh, I see, miss. You're looking to split hairs. I could tell just by looking at the bastard he was gaming the system. That work better for you? But, see, his license looked real and he was paying cash. Business is business at the end of the day."

"In forty years you never rented this place to anyone from the wrong side of the tracks?"

"What do you mean this place?"

Rebecca gives a look like Come on, man, look around you, but holds silent.

The manager brushes it aside. "Could afford to be choosy before the freeway. Back then, people had to drive right through the center of town. Now . . ." he trails off and his eyes swing back to the photo on the counter. He lashes out and slaps it with the back of his hand, as if Paul is directly responsible for the motel's economic misfortunes.

Rebecca's hands are stuffed deep inside her pockets. She watches his tantrum through bored, dispassionate eyes. Thinks, Just give me something I can use . . .

Without lunch in her stomach, her head continues to throb.

The manager finishes thrashing the photo and she takes it back, asks to see the room.

"Better I show you," he says. "Otherwise you'll be back down here in five seconds asking me what happened to it."

"That would be fine."

"Ain't touching squat in there until the insurance company gets its ass out here to look. I mean, Jesus H. Christ on a popsicle stick, you think they can fit me into their busy schedule?" He steps out from behind the counter and storms past, shoving through the office door without waiting for her to follow.

Rebecca has to hurry to catch up. "So he was here for three days?"

"Seven. Paid by the day. Except for the last three. Son of a bitch . . ."

"He alone?"

"Had a girl with him on a few nights. At least one."

The room's directly upstairs. The manager uses his universal keycard to open it up. Then he stands aside, leaving Rebecca to enter alone. She hears the flick of a BIC lighter at her back. Erratic footsteps begin to pace the wooden landing, leaving her to take it all in.

What a mess.

Paul, she thinks, and finds a shark's grin on her face. I'm close and I bet you don't even know it. Her mind may be jelly, but there's the one thing that stands out. Finding him.

The smell is the first thing that strikes. She puts the back of her hand against her nose as she sweeps the room.

Shattered mirrors. A small camping hatchet cleaved straight through the plasma screen, where only the metal hilt juts out from the center crack. Clothes are strewn everywhere. Some his. Some belonging to women. Also possibly his, she guesses, though her gut is suddenly adamant against that conclusion. He liked girls too damn much.

How in the hell can you know that for sure? she thinks.

More people than just Paul have been here. That's the only way to explain the sheer volume of shit smears decorating these walls.

It's everywhere. Rubbed in long comet streaks. Splatters on the inside windows like exploded brown snowballs. It's ground into the rug like hardened gum. Different shades of brown and green soil the ceiling, various colors and consistencies. You have to drink a lot of coffee and maw through at least a dozen fast food value menus before your movements start looking this unhealthy.

Understandably, this sight is the trigger for Mr. Manager, who remains planted on the porch, peering in to see if it's really as bad as his memory. Oh, it is. He screams "fucking savages" without an ounce of regard for his other patrons.

The shit has symbols carved in it. Each of these markings impressed by fingertip. Rebecca doesn't recognize the language.

"In there," the manager says, half his tilted head visible. His limp wrist flicks toward the bathroom.

"But all the shit's out here," Rebecca says dryly and then goes to check. The bathroom floor is coated in ash. Burnt paper crunches like fresh fallen snow. She braces herself for the worst as she leans over the tub. Even more ash. Mounds upon mounds of it. Nothing salvageable. Or readable.

"You said he had a girl up here with him," she calls. "At least one. Know who she was?"

"Cassie Pennington," he growls. "And I'd take the money out of her ass if her family had a pot to piss in."

"Then you know where they live."

"Ain't gonna do you much good," he says. "Crazy bitch has been under house arrest since . . ."

"Since what?"

"Christ," he says, growing really irritated with her ignorance. "You don't know?"

Rebecca gives him her most exasperated face. She's too tired, too miserable for this tête-à-tête.

"Your missing person's a bad guy," he says.

Rebecca thinks of Jaime lying on that slab, every shade of blue inside the crayon box and with half her face cut away. She mounts her hands on her hips because, yes, that's obvious.

"He and his jailbait girlfriend killed a few people."

"A few?"

The manager turns his index finger downward. "Here in town," he says. "Shit, that was a month back now."

That sounds impossible. How could she not know something like that? But the more she thinks on it, on her recent situation and the way the orderlies there tried to keep information from her, Rebecca realizes that anything's possible.

She's got her phone. Researching won't be hard, but what's the point? What's done is done. She's just looking to mop up.

"Give me Cassie's address."

The manager gives general directions, says it won't be hard to find because there's nothing out that way and I mean nothing. Rebecca types it into her phone. "Appreciate your time," she says, stepping back out into the frosty air. Her breastbone radiates more heat than a furnace in February.

"Who hired you?" he calls from the landing above, still puffing smoke into the afternoon air.

"Book me a room," she says. "Be back later." She gets into her car without answering the question.

6

REBECCA DRIVES OUT TO THE middle of nowhere and finds an old saltbox sitting in a field of tall grass. Warped wood, chipped paint, cracked windows. It's old and dilapidated and to pass it from the road would make one think it's been abandoned since the days when horse-drawn sleds carried people into town.

Rebecca thinks the address has to be wrong. Thinks this because clearly nobody's lived here for decades. Nobody seems to live out this way at all. She hasn't seen another vehicle for miles. And the old Ford junker that sits beside the house up there doesn't count, all rusted and nearly swallowed whole by eager grass.

But then she catches a flicker in the window. A pulled curtain and, beyond it, a curious onlooker who stands in the form of a shadow peering out. The fabric falls back into place as soon as this person realizes someone's out there, staring right back.

Movement's movement, Rebecca thinks. It emboldens her to turn in on the driveway and coast toward the rickety porch. The car buckles on unkempt terrain, dirt and stone, and once she reaches the house, she kills the engine and steps outside. The world around her goes silent with the suddenness of an off switch.

Not so much as a single chirping bird or fluttering insect wing to score the afternoon. A crucified scarecrow with its back to her stands a silent sentry against the far-off tree line, a couple of hundred feet back. There's no farmland here that she can see, which makes its presence, and direction, off-kilter and odd.

The porch is even worse beneath her feet. Spots of softened, almost entirely rotted wood. It wobbles and bends under her boot heels. It takes six knocks on the door for someone to answer. A woman with a long face and an even longer cigarette perched between thin lips. She matches Rebecca's age, roughly, and has the bored eyes of a housewife well beyond her usefulness.

Rebecca empathizes with that empty gaze, but common ground's short-lived. The woman spits a yellow glob of emphysema at her feet and says "What" without a trace of interrogation.

"Cassie home?"

The woman flings the door wide and shambles out. Leans in on Rebecca's face, scrunching close enough to see her pores. "Hell you want her for?"

"Questions."

"She hasn't been out since . . . since the last time."

Rebecca lifts her hands in surrender, hoping to ease the tension before it goes airborne. "Just here to talk," she says. "About . . . last time."

The woman backs off, retreats and leaves the door wide as she heads for the parlor off to the left. Hideous flower-patterned wallpaper runs all the way to the ceiling, where it peels at the corners, forcing a few of the larger flaps to lean downward.

The woman says nothing more, points to the center staircase as she sits stoic on the garish couch. The cushions are so depressed she nearly falls through to the floor.

Every step creaks like a rusty hinge. Gotta be impossible to sneak out of this place. The air in here's thick, like breathing syrup. Cigarette stench lives inside everything, even the wood, and a thick sheet of resting dust is settled atop every surface. People live here now, but this place is already auditioning to be a haunted house.

The girl who has to be Cassie Pennington stands in the doorway of her bedroom, smiling broadly as if she'd been posed there all day, just waiting for someone to come calling. Cassie's jailbait so blatant you'd have to register as a sex offender just for looking at her wrong. A billowy nightgown clings to her curves, inviting gazes. An electric monitor is strapped to her ankle.

Rebecca speaks first. "I'm–"

"Don't matter who y'are," she says. Retreats inside her room and leaves the door wide open.

This is what passes for manners in this house.

Rebecca enters and stays against the wall, watching as the girl moves to the barred window across the way. She's backlit there by enough sunlight to render her gown see-through.

Cassie's well built. Large breasts, wide hips, and a behind that curves like sculpted porcelain. Has the kind of pin-up look usually reserved for calendars that hang inside garages on oil-smeared walls.

Rebecca gets lost in the sight. Not lustfully, but because she remembers yesterday like it was yesterday. A stab of nostalgia slices her as she realizes just how long ago yesterday was. So much wasted time between then and now. Dreams given to other dreams, resulting in promises unfulfilled.

And now here Rebecca is, mid-forties and carrying envy for a girl who can't legally drive.

Cassie catches this gaze and smiles at the attention while Rebecca stays lost in the memories. She remembers what it was like to turn heads this way. For her, it had been her long, tanned legs sheathed in late 80s running shorts. Dark blue and bordered white, stamped with the embroidered logo of a prowling puma. She looked good in those. Used to hike them up an extra inch as soon as she hit the sidewalk, for the confidence, jogging and greeting each neighborly wave with a blasé grin. Innocent, but deliberate. Life then was wide open and limitless.

Rebecca's still got her assets, each day's a fight against age and gravity–and those bastards come constantly to try and take them.

"Not gonna find him, you know," Cassie says.

Rebecca snaps out of the daydream and asks, "Who?"

"Quit it, bitch. You're standing in my room checking out my tits. Least you can do is be real with me."

"Paul," Rebecca says, embarrassed that her mind has wandered so far away. "You're talking about Paul."

Cassie nods expectantly at the mention but her eyes swivel toward the window. Stares down at the distant scarecrow as she remembers the truth. Truth she's never going to give.

"Where did he go?" Rebecca asks.

Cassie turns. One blink and she's back from her own nostalgic trip. "Hm?"

"You're so sure I'm not going to find him. I'd like to know where he went."

"That's the thing," Cassie's voice is airy now, with a playful inflection that's maybe a little mocking, though Rebecca doesn't think so. She's just nuts. "I don't know where he went. Only know that he's gone . . . gone, baby, gone."

"So tell me what you do know."

Cassie rubs her eyes with the back of her hand. "I know everything's going to be different now. I know that I'm not going to see him again."

"How does that make you feel?"

"Knock it off, okay? If you wanna know what we were, why don't you just ask?"

"Okay," Rebecca says. "I'm asking."

The girl shrugs, glides over to her bureau from across the room. She checks herself in the empty frame sitting atop it. The spot where a mirror should be, though the girl doesn't appear to notice it's missing. "He liked fucking me. Whatever passes for fun in this part of the world, right?"

"That passes for fun everywhere."

Cassie gives a knowing point like at last they've found common ground. "Right? Universal language."

"You weren't boyfriend and girlfriend?"

"Cute, Mom. Call us whatever you want. I give a fuck?"

"And you stayed in the Harvest Hill Motor Inn?"

"Not all the time. We liked new places. Tried lots of them."

"Adventurous."

"I guess." Cassie shrugs like she's never thought of it that way. This isn't a girl who cares much about what the world around her has to say about anything. "Mostly just wanted him to put a baby in me. Guy like that . . . you do what you gotta do to lock him down. Keeping things unpredictable keeps them rock hard. And public places are exciting. You do what you can. Bet you had guys like that in your day?"

"Ever try the beach?"

A smile like she's swapping naughty secrets at a sleepover. "Once or twice. Ocean's too far away to do it more than that."

Rebecca is suddenly enraged. Her pulse quickens and her heart's wedged in her throat. Doesn't know how Cassie has managed to breach her armor with something so trivial, but the anger builds with surprising momentum. She feels like snatching this little cunt and squeezing her windpipe until the truth comes oozing from her ears like mashed potatoes.

It's at last a thought that brings genuine humor to her face.

Rebecca knows she shouldn't care so much about this girl's sex life, so long as she gets answers. But rage burns through her like wildfire. In a bout of misplaced callousness, she resists the urge to tell her that Paul's heart belonged to another. It's hard to imagine something that could be more antithetical to her purpose, though, so she shifts gears and says, "I saw the hotel room."

"Looked like shit," the girl laughs. "Didn't it?"

"What did you do in there?"

"Said goodbye."

"So . . . he left you?"

"He left."

"Where did he go?"

"On ahead. For Tanner Red."

That sounds like some campaign slogan. Rebecca asks after it, but the girl only slides over to her bed and sits. Her back arches and her fiery red hair unfurls and dances like the spitting blaze from an inverse campfire. She stares at Rebecca invitingly, scissoring her exposed and sweaty thighs.

"What's the last thing he said to you?" Rebecca says.

Cassie laughs, closes her eyes and chuckles soft. She enjoys the memory first inside her own head. Eyes flutter and lift and she smiles. "It'll sound crazy."

We're past crazy, Rebecca thinks. What Rebecca says is, "Try me."

"He said, 'It's been fun.'"

The girl shuts down at that, stretching out on the bed and shutting her eyes, rolling wantonly above the sheets.

That's as much help as Cassie's willing to be. Rebecca leaves back down the groaning steps. Passes the girl's mother on the couch. The woman stares up at a water stain on the ceiling that's spreading in real time. Small drips pluck down on the hardwood. It takes the woman a long while to blink even once, but she never looks again at the stranger in her house.

"Is your daughter all right?" Rebecca asks.

"No," she says with barely any pitch. "Been wrong for as long as I can remember."

"I can ask after some counseling when I get back into—"

"Counseling can't fix this."

Rebecca starts inside the room, prepared to argue. To make the case that yes, it can, but she gets as far as the threshold and pauses at the sight of the mirror hanging on the back wall, the room reflecting right back. Mostly. Rebecca isn't in the image. In her place stands a girl splattered in so much blood a year's worth of hot showers wouldn't be able to wash it all away.

The whites of the girl's eyes stand out with so much definition it's like they're glowing. Rebecca takes a step back, startled. The girl in the mirror moves toward the frame and her face never comes further into focus, even as her body nears.

On the couch, the mother doesn't seem to notice any of this.

The reflected girl takes another step forward, even as Rebecca stands sedentary. The glass starts to ripple and bend, almost like expanding lungs.

Rebecca rushes for the door, certain she doesn't want to see what happens next.

7

ONCE MORE SHE GLIMPSES THE scarecrow at the far edge of the Pennington property.

Rather than go to her car, Rebecca starts toward the high grass. She walks until the house over her shoulder is the size of a dollhouse.

The scarecrow looms large. Rebecca looks up at the display. Its clothes are crisp—fresh off the store shelf. Something about the way its plaid shirt is tucked into bright blue denim jeans . . .

The tongues of its unspoiled Timberlands are spattered in blood and there's a stitch of space where the gloves meet the sleeve. Tight loops of frayed rope have sunk through darkened flesh there . . .

The last few buttons of its shirt are separated and propped open to reveal bales of red-stained hay.

Sitting atop the grotesque display isn't a sackcloth face, but instead the severed head of a real sheep. Blank onyx eyes are ever vigilant against the unseen horrors of the woods.

Whatever this is fills her with overwhelming dread. A god-awful tableau that somehow proves there's nothing positive in this world, for how can there be when something so nightmarish stands?

Rebecca rushes back to her car, realizes she's running full sprint. She happens to glance up at the house as she reaches it. Cassie stands in the window there, wearing a smile so wide they'd see it on the moon. She seems freshly charged after watching Rebecca high tail it across her back yard.

Cassie's bare breasts mash against the glass with enough force to turn her smooshed skin three shades lighter. Her lips fall on the pane next, growing her mouth into a monstrous caricature. She grinds against it, thrusting her hips at Rebecca in a mocking but obscene gesture.

Rebecca gets into the car, gives the ignition a flick and catches the girl flipping the finger as she reverses toward the road, trying to forget all about that awful scarecrow. And even worse, that reflection in the mirror.

She wishes to forget everything except for Cassie's most curious words.

"On ahead. For Tanner Red."

She hits the pavement, glad to leave the whole awful house in her blacked-out, duct-tape-covered rearview.

8

THE MIGRAINE RETURNS AROUND DUSK while Rebecca sits in her car, scrolling her phone to brush up on Bright Fork's recent killings.

She's parked in the empty library lot, not quite ready to cloister herself inside her motel room for the evening, when the pain comes at her like the swing of a sledgehammer. Hits her so hard the phone goes tumbling from her hand and slips beneath the seat.

She usually goes straight for her Advil. This time she goes right for her eyes, pressing at her temples with the rounds of her hands. This pain's a goddamn lightning bolt. She twists like a pretzel in uncontrollable spasms. She stretches blindly for the Advil, fingers propped wide, but her body's in open revolt, muscles refusing to comply.

Rebecca catches sight of her reflection in the darkened windshield and screams bloody murder. It's so loud several passersby squint through the night for a better look.

"Oh God," Rebecca cries, looking at the face overlaid on her reflection. Her head moves to one side, ear slamming against shoulder bone. The stranger's face remains locked dead center. It stares back, unmoved, like a frozen image on a plasma television screen. The same face in the glass at Cassie Pennington's house, still obscured by foggy glass and softer vision.

Burgundy tears roll from the stranger's ducts like mini red carpets. Runny trails on reflected cheeks. But Rebecca feels those same wet tickles crawling down her face, coasting straight for her mouth on sunken age lines. Her tongue flicks out and catches a bitter sting as if to prove to her brain this is real.

A startled gasp as her vision cuts out, leaving her to feel around in sudden darkness.

Panic now that she's gone blind. Her fingers find the door handle. She shoves it outward and falls toward pavement.

That reflected face haunts the darkness behind her eyelids. It's a youthful, red smile that grins wide in spite of its terrible appearance. Blood seeps through the marginal gaps in her teeth. But it's the whites of those eyes . . . missing pupils that take away the only bit of humanity it could have.

"Jesus, girly, c'mere." Hands around Rebecca's shoulders. Frail and flexing arms that barely get her back to her feet. Around her, voices debate:

"Call the sheriff."

"Not the sheriff. Call an ambulance."

"She don't need either . . . get her to a loony bin." The bloody face laughs at this suggestion and it's a sick, percussive sound.

Rebecca is too disoriented to settle on any one thing. The sting of open air slows her heart and her vision returns like a warming projector bulb.

She thinks, I'll never take it for granted again.

Now she's worried about the flurry of concerned faces hovering inside her personal bubble. Feels like half the fucking town's leaning into her face, huddled way too close, as if proximity holds the answers.

"No," Rebecca says. She whirls around to study her reflection in the car window. Her fingertips crawl her cheeks and find dry flesh. A little chapped, but dry. The blood's a memory.

"I'll be fine," she tells no one in particular. This assurance is for her. These people don't care one iota for her well-being. She knows that.

Rebecca slips back behind the wheel as the townspeople close in around her hood like the professional gawkers they are. They're in a semi-circle, prying through the glass.

She holds up the Advil and shakes the bottle, as if that explains or excuses her condition.

Then she starts the car and reverses the hell out of there, smashing the pedal.

She's barely out of the parking lot when red and blues explode behind her.

9

BEFORE TODAY, REBECCA HAS NEVER been inside of a jail cell.

This may be considered odd, given her line of work, but she never had to walk anyone to the iron. And almost all of her business these days is done outside police stations. Law enforcement views her profession as a one-way street with almost nothing to gain from cooperation. In fact, it's usually nil.

Rebecca used to have a few sources stemming back to her time on the force. When she wanted nothing more than to make detective. Right before the reality of motherhood put that dream on hold. And once it was time to get back to the shield, Bret decided to leverage their little girl as a bargaining chip in order to keep her out of the most dangerous profession.

Massachusetts State Police was going to have to find a detective elsewhere.

Rebecca went into private investigation and never looked back. The hours are hers, the beat, not as unforgiving. Her clients are mostly lawyers and insurance adjustors, along with the occasional private citizen who thinks his or her spouse has taken up spurious nocturnal activities.

The cell is small, cramped. About as comfortable as the shitty motel she'll be staying at if she ever gets out of here.

The sheriff sits upfront, reading a newspaper that's constantly wrinkling. He realizes Rebecca is stirring and reaches for something out of view. Comes down the way and passes a Styrofoam container through the bars. Three tacos. Corn tortillas soggy from too much melted cheese and greasy beef.

Rebecca goes at it anyway, chomping like it's her first meal in ages.

"Can't stand all the Americana the diner serves," the sheriff says. He's Hispanic, judging from the way the tip of his tongue curls his words as he talks. Of course, the nametag that reads CORTEZ is the real tip off.

"Wouldn't kill them to have a taco truck," Rebecca says, spraying greasy beef all over the cell. "Chinese takeout. Falafel. Something."

The sheriff laughs. It's the first time she's heard anyone in this miserable town do that. "No, it wouldn't. I gotta go all the way to Pontiac for authentic Mexican."

Rebecca lifts her taco like it's a beer. "Cheers."

"Wasn't originally for you. My deputy's out sick."

"Either way." The hammering headache recedes the more she eats. After all three tacos are decimated, she licks grease and hot sauce off her lips, picking up little hunks of beef and shredded lettuce between her fingers and then licking them too.

"Cortez," he says and sticks his hand through the bars.

Rebecca places the empty container at her feet and shakes with her clean hand. The wrong hand. The sheriff laughs again. He opens the cell and turns his back, a motion that proves he's a trusting person.

"Town's worried about you," he says.

"That's nice." She steps out and follows.

"You have a permit for your weapon, so I'm not too concerned about that. More private citizens should exercise their 2A rights . . . you get me."

"I do." She doesn't.

"And you've got enough Advil to stock a pharmacy. That's really none of mine, either, but let me tell you what is."

Rebecca goes to the sheriff's desk. What's coming is due. She knew she could only run for so long, and with her newfound ailments getting worse, what could she expect?

It was always going to end this way. She only wishes she could've found Paul first.

She slumps into the chair that faces the desk and prepares for the hammer to fall. The escaped mental patient is going back, and this time it'll be anything but voluntary admission.

Cortez sits with his legs up. Hands on the back of his head because this is still the easy life from where he sits. Small towns are usually about as dangerous as pre-school recess. Except this small town has suffered three murders. "You're carrying a picture of a missing person," he says.

"I know that."

"Someone who disappeared from these parts. Someone this town would like to find."

"Me too."

A nervous smile. "You think he's still here?"

"Trail goes cold." Rebecca points out the window, realizes she doesn't know where the hotel sits in relation to this place, but the effect stands. "Goes cold in that hotel room."

"So you're done? Wrapping up?"

"Not even close."

Cortez comes down off his perch. The chair squeaks as he spins to face her directly. This is what he wants to hear.

Rebecca gets it. He's gotta be careful. She tries to understand that, but time's wasting. And if he isn't going to call the hospital and send her back, then cut her loose. She can't say that though, because she's not sure that's the game they're playing. So she stares back with wide eyes to show she doesn't have the time to be yanking any chains.

He takes a deep breath. "I'm going to toss you back," he says. Taps her revolver sitting on his desk. "This stays with me, though."

Rebecca cocks her head. Looks around. The station's empty save for the two of them and a dispatcher in the next office filing her nails. If this is a trap, it doesn't feel that way to her gut.

Cortez reads the question in her eyes. "No catch," he says. "Not if you think you can deliver him."

"I intend to."

"If it gets out that I let you walk, and you do something stupid, they'll run me out of town with you. But I read up on you. I think you can do it."

"Is that right?"

"Call me a fan."

"Not going to ask me to sign an autograph, are you?"

Cortez smiles wryly. "No," he says, but something in his eyes shows he might've been thinking about it. "But I have THE Rebecca Daniels in my station. In another life, I'd want to talk shop."

A shrug as she says, "I just did my job."

"You would say it like that." Cortez smirks. "So would I. They don't train us for it, do they?"

"Train us for what?"

"All the hero talk. If you don't squirm when you hear it, then your mindset ain't right. Nobody likes a superstar in this line of work."

Rebecca takes a deep breath. Cortez is right about that. She's never liked talking about herself. "I just want to close this out."

He tosses his card and it lands in her lap. "You find him, you give me a call." His eyes dip to the gun. "Maybe I'll give that back to you then."

Maybe, Rebecca thinks. Or maybe I'll just kill him with whatever's handy and then disappear before you decide to pin your vigilantism on me. Paul doesn't need to be pumped full of bullets in order to die. After the things he's done, a bullet's almost too quick. More than revenge, she wants him to feel every ounce of the pound she's fixing to carve from his flesh.

The chair squeaks as she pushes away from the desk. That should be that, but Cortez isn't content to let her go just yet. She sees from the disappointment in his eyes that his little show of faith was meant to spur conversation.

"I'm not here to make friends," she says.

"Who'd you lose?" Cortez thinks he can salvage this, motions for her to sit.

Rebecca is halfway to the door.

"Okay," he says with a tightening jaw. He turns toward the window so he can see Bright Fork. The view is probably a constant reminder of his enduring failure to serve and protect. "My kid sister."

"Shit," she says. "I'm sorry."

"Me too. The way she died—" Cortez catches himself before his voice cracks. Takes another pause while Rebecca stands helpless. This wretched sight awakens something in her. She fights the urge to touch him with a mother's hands. Pass along what little comfort she can provide. But those instincts are from so long ago they're almost alien to her now.

A dream of another life.

"Skin was all they left of her. Deflated like a popped balloon. Don't even know what they did with her bones ... her organs ... never found any of them ..."

Rebecca's jaw tightens. "She deserves justice."

"So does he. Paul."

"Paul's going to get it. Where was this?"

"Herbert Farm, out on Brockleman Road. But forget about it. We've been through that place time and time again. I had forensics camped out there for a week. Checked every acre twice."

"Paul and Cassie killed others, too."

"Knew you were good," Cortez says.

Rebecca doesn't want to get his hopes up. He already seems to think a superhero has come waltzing into town in order to help with his problem. "Somebody literally told me," she says.

"Still, been in town, what? Half a day? We've got three victims total. Plenty of debate on what Cassie knows and what she actually did. Two psychologists have given her a victim's profile. Hear them tell it, her mind's warped and Paul just affected her in a different way. Attorneys are keeping her out of the straight jacket for now. Monitoring bracelet ain't enough, you ask me, but whatever keeps her out of Bright Fork proper ..."

After her visit, Rebecca thinks it's easy to imagine Cassie being knee-deep in these killings. It doesn't take a hypnotist to make a teenage girl do something crazy in the name of love when her brain has already short-circuited. "Tell me about the other two murders." She was beginning to research them when the headache struck. Rebecca doesn't want to think about that now.

"Father Kindry out at St. Cecilia's. I don't even know what to say about that one. Melted the church tabernacle and poured it down his throat. Left him on the altar for Sunday mass, dead five days."

"Animals," she says.

"Third was a night nurse, Marci Rooker, on her way home in the early morning. Looks like Paul staged car trouble and clipped her the second she stopped." Hopeless laughter scrapes his throat. "That's what being a Good Samaritan gets you."

"And you can't find him?"

"I've looked," Cortez says. Suddenly she's aware of all the empty Styrofoam cups stacked in the waste bin beside his desk. The deep stubble growing out of his cheeks. The raccoon circles that look drawn on with Sharpie beneath his eyes. "All I do is look."

"You're not looking in the right place," she says.

"What does that mean?"

"I don't know yet."

Cortez looks at her hard so there's no mistaking it. Sanctioned violence passes unspoken between them. Rebecca lets that settle inside her heart. She's already got stone cold hatred pumping through all four chambers. If she can take a little heat off the sheriff, that's a burden she's willing to shoulder. Thinks maybe she is a superhero, after all.

Because not everyone needs to be fluent in this type of grief.

"One last thing," he says.

She only pauses, doesn't turn.

"This town looks to me to protect it. Your history, your troubles . . . I'm taking a chance on letting you walk."

"You are," she says. "Because you want this too. His death is the only thing that keeps you going."

"Yes."

"It's better than any other motivation. Nothing distracts from that kind of focus."

"I know."

"I'm going to find him."

"Just don't–"

"I won't." Rebecca doesn't even know what he was about to say. It doesn't matter.

Cortez stands and Rebecca pauses in the doorway to ensure he hasn't changed his mind. "Oh yeah," he says. "Your side mirrors are broken off. Your rearview mirror was wrapped in duct tape. Had to undo that, at least. Safety issue. I'm responsible for all roads in and through this town so . . . well, I'm sure you understand."

She leaves without another word.

10

FIRST THING SHE DOES WHEN she gets to the car is tear the entire rearview mirror off its mount and stuff it inside the garbage can across the street.

Her hands are soaking wet with runny soot as she hurries back across the crosswalk.

11

"BECKS . . . WHERE ARE YOU?"

"Someplace warm."

"Where?"

"Key West. You've seen pictures."

"You're bullshitting me."

"Never."

"You're on the run? Never going to come in?"

"I'm bullshitting. Remember?"

"Goddammit, why? Why do you always do this?"

"Nothing left to do."

"Let it go. I still need you."

"Can't."

"Tell me where you are so I can help."

"You mean so you can send the cops to pick me up."

"Becks–"

"The cops here understand. Better than you."

"How can you say I don't understand?"

"Truth's painful."

"You don't even know what the truth is anymore. That's why you've got me on speed dial. Any more dreams you need vetted, or is your brain working again?"

"Remember the macaroni lion?"

"Yes," Bret says. "Goddamn right I do. Jaime's picture that you hung over the dining room table."

"Yeah, well, better than the canned art you buy at Home Goods."

"You dreamt about the macaroni lion?"

"No. I remember it."

"I don't follow."

"I remember the day she made it. Fusilli for the lion's mane. Her idea. What was she? Seven? I was so proud. Couldn't wait to see where life took her. She was always good at finding her own path. At putting her stamp on things."

"I know, there's a million of those memories . . ."

"You never understood."

"I understand you're obsessed. And talking to me about macaroni lions."

"Fuck off."

"Don't put this on me. You broke Benny's nose."

"He tried to stop me."

"Jesus Christ . . . is that a threat?"

"Not if you don't try and stop me."

"Jesus Christ."

Rebecca hangs up and tosses the phone atop the bed. She considers turning it off for the night, but it doesn't matter.

She sits on the table with a glass of melted ice in her hand. The water's tepid but it tastes good. Still manages to cool her heated insides.

Around her, the room's mirrors are blotted. Her sweatshirt is draped across the bathroom vanity while the bed's comforter is stretched tight to cover the head-to-floor piece.

The temperature control keeps her skin perpetually cool and pocked by gooseflesh. She's nude because she no longer trusts her body and prefers to keep an eye on it whenever the curtains are drawn and the doors are locked.

Sometimes at night her legs itch and she scratches them red in her sleep. Sometimes it's worse. On the night of her escape there was a moment of panic that drove her to freedom. She sprung up in bed to find her breasts had doubled in size while her hands, appropriately aged and veiny for a woman fast-approaching 50, had smoothed into that of a woman's less than half her age.

And you don't take those symptoms to the doctor, otherwise you wind up right back in Straightjacket City.

When that stuff happens, the mirrors show you the truth. Except, the mirrors have turned against her. Rebecca no longer looks at them.

She fears that something lives inside her. Something that splits her brain in two and makes reality feel like it's always a dream away. Whatever's happened, whatever's doing this, makes life feel like a fever.

Beneath the bathroom mirror comes the tapping. That one slow clinking fingernail patters the glass. An indifferent jangle that makes her feel achingly helpless, almost numb to the sound.

She thinks about the six-shooter and remembers her new pal Cortez is holding it for her. Can't help but wonder whether or not she'd turn the gun on herself in this weak moment. Cash out forever. Or keep to the trail because it's hot and she's close. Too close to quit.

Will Paul even remember? Why do we assume we leave such little impression on others? Rebecca worries about that because she's spent the last year trying to imagine the look on his face once he realizes it's her who's come to put him down. And she knows he must be out there somewhere expecting it.

Her phone leaps back to life with another silent glow. She envisions Bret hunched over his phone, oversized fingers tapping QWERTY glass. The image uncouples her train of thought. She laughs cruelly, even as persistent tapping glass reminds her nothing's funny anymore. She crosses the room on bare feet. The thin carpet freezes her soles, but it's a refreshing ripple through her baking body.

"Let us look." A gravel-laden voice says, nearly atonal and muffled beneath blotted mirrors. "Let us see."

Rebecca rushes to the phone, snatches it off the bed. She doesn't want Bret's nagging words but has never heard voices beyond the glass. This part's new. The game's changing. Faster since arriving in Bright Fork.

The migraine returns with tremors. So much pain she wants to die.

Her forehead itches. She touches her fingers to the surface there and finds small mounds of flesh jutting outward. Little beads that feel like full-headed pimples, raw to the touch. Breathing pustules, startling enough to force a shriek from her throat.

Her scream startles the room into silence.

The pain's gone.

So are the voices.

Everything except the tapping.

That never stops.

Rebecca reaches for the bourbon.

12

UNDERNEATH TAPPING MIRRORS WAITS A dream.

Rebecca sleeps on the floor in a makeshift bed of mottled sheets—a situation better suited for a family dog they never got around to having. Her mouth is dry like sun-beat sand and the empty pint of Wild Turkey leaks noxious fumes into the air.

And still, the dream slips through. It comes with arms like blankets, swaddling her inside comfortable memories:

The macaroni lion.

Thursday diner dives with Jaime.

Driver's ed practice sessions—one in particular where Jaime slammed the gas instead of the brakes and obliterated the Bartons' prized petunias and part of their picket fence in the process.

Two weeks at Disney World when Jaime was nine and thought Mickey Mouse was her bestie.

Sleepless Christmas Eves, Jaime worried what would happen if Santa couldn't figure out how to get inside the house since they had no fireplace.

See that, Rebecca thinks. I had a real life once.

She tosses over. Fluttering eyes find the motel wall one inch from her nose and Rebecca thinks nothing of it. Her bourbon-soaked brain is anchored to the void, eyelids closing fast.

The dream returns before she even realizes it's missing.

And now she's settled into another memory.

This one's got the sweet-sour smell of lemonade. It colors the air with nostalgia. A tall woman moves in irregular, jagged time, like frames cut haphazardly from a film reel. She jump cuts all the way down the porch steps and vanishes just before reaching the cornfield. Long stalks wobble in the spot where her body disappeared.

Rebecca watches from the porch and feels compelled to follow. From the house, a gathering speaks in distorted trumpets. Charlie Brown adults who're saying nothing she wants to hear. She peers in through the screen door and finds only people-shaped shadows projected across a distant kitchen wall. Clanking plates, scraping forks, muted and careful laughter—all of it out of reach.

Forever just around the corner.

The cornfield's preferable.

Rebecca moves toward it. Anything to get away from that warbling crowd. Anyplace they can't follow. The one place they won't go.

She remembers this day in vivid color. You always do when it's one of your parents who goes.

Rebecca doesn't need Bret to validate this. Maybe the hospital tried to make her forget things, but this is safe and secure inside her soul. The death of her mother at fifty-seven years of age, cut to the bone by a double dose of ovarian and breast cancer.

Poor woman never stood a chance.

Rebecca has never forgotten her mother's last words. The doctor had just briefed them on prolonged treatment and felt hospice was premature. As soon as they were alone, Mom reached up, took Rebecca's wrist and spent the next five minutes conjuring the energy to speak. It came out sounding like gravel, but Mom was determined to spit every syllable. "Ain't putting my family through any more of this. I'm dead no matter what I do. Last gift I can give is to punch out tonight. Only way to do it, as far as I can see."

She was dead twelve hours later, resolute in her decision to spare her family an onslaught of future headaches.

Funerals are tough. Everyone wants to know how you're doing. They come offering comfort and consolation they can't actually give. They want to share memories of the departed because that's what they came to do and believe in their hearts that you need to hear every word they've got on the subject.

Rebecca doesn't want any of that. What she wants is five minutes to herself. And that's where the corn comes in. She follows the flickering woman as the stalks slap gently against her face.

The woman in a mourning dress kneels on tamped earth, staring up at the sky. Streaks of mascara shimmer in the sunlight, making it look like she's crying tar.

The woman turns at the sound of an approaching body.

Familiar words come out of her in Rebecca's voice. "Can you not?"

Rebecca stops dead, unable to process this. Those are her words and not for this stranger to steal.

Still, the stranger continues, "Jesus Christ. My mother is dead, and you can't give me five fucking minutes to process it? Five minutes to think about her without you bothering me?"

Rebecca starts toward the stranger with arms outstretched.

The stranger doesn't want her. "Can't your father get you juice? Play with you? Tell you what's for dinner? What do you need me for? Can you please just leave me the hell alone?"

But Rebecca needs a hug. Continues forward, arms wide. The stranger doesn't want it, tries to push her back. "Get away from me," she growls, aiming for Rebecca's shoulder. But her aim's off, and that misplaced hand cracks Rebecca in the nose, sends her stuttering back, falling on crushed stalks.

And then Rebecca's memory is back where it belongs. It's her kneeling on the dead stalks, looking into the runny eyes of her eight-year-old daughter. Blood drips from Jaime's nose. She looks hurt and terrified because Mom has never snapped at her this way.

"Jaime," Rebecca starts.

Way too late. Jaime turns and rushes back toward the house,

stalks ruffling like ripples in a pond as she goes. The only time Mom ever hit her.

The dream says Jaime remembers it even today, stunned her mother could be so cruel.

Rebecca has never felt lower. She falls against the corn as the sobs come on hard and seemingly never stop.

To this day, that betrayal in her daughter's eyes is the thing she regrets most.

13

THE "GET BLACKOUT DRUNK" METHOD isn't foolproof, Rebecca learns.

She sits with her knees against her chest, squinting against the encroaching sun that tries breaking through the spaces around the drawn shades.

Last night's dream has shaken her.

She rises and stretches to get the crimps out of her back. This kind of sleep isn't sleep and she feels somehow worse for even trying. She showers and dresses and brushes her teeth twice to exorcise the bourbon stink from the back of her throat. That's no use. She's going to be suffering that awful taste on her tongue for a long time.

She craves chicken and waffles. All the maple syrup she can stand.

She places the DO NOT DISTURB placard on the doorknob and calls down to the front desk. Last thing she wants is some unsuspecting maid coming in here to yank the sheets down off the mirrors.

"What kind of a request is that?" the manager demands.

She assures him she won't be smearing shit all over the walls. "I just like my privacy," she says.

"I don't really care what you do," he tells her. "It's why I charged you double. Security deposit. New policy. If I find shit on your walls, you don't get it back."

She cracks the door and sunlight stings. Has to slip behind her Ray-Bans to weather that discomfort, because this is going to be a long day.

"Still don't know who hired you." The manager stands in the office doorway. She gets the sense the old pervert likes to watch her leave because he does exactly that. Stares at her ass from over the coffee mug tipped against his mouth.

Rebecca drops into the driver's seat. Glances at her phone out of habit and finds a thread of unread messages from Bret, all of them fixing to talk her out of this.

She deletes them without reading and turns the ignition.

14

REBECCA FINDS HERBERT FARM NESTLED firmly into the middle of nowhere. The door opens with a cowbell clink as she pushes inside the general store. The place is all wood panels, impeccable produce piled into wicker baskets. Homemade shelving displays a pyramid of Herbert-branded salad dressings and marinades. Newman's Own has got nothing on these folks.

The register is unmanned. This part of the world is just that trusting. Even after murder comes knocking, it still trusts.

Rebecca makes the rounds, browsing and enjoying air sweeter than a bakery. The back counter is stocked with fresh meat pies.

"Can I help you?"

A young woman appears through swinging kitchen doors carrying two more steaming pies. She places them next to the others and shoos Rebecca away, as if she's going to sew her germs inside the settling crusts.

Rebecca flashes the photo of Paul like it's a police badge. "Did you know him?"

The girl suddenly looks like her day's ruined. "No. Don't know him. But I know who he is."

"Who is he?"

"Killed the sheriff's sister . . . those others . . ."

"Know where he is?"

She doesn't bother to answer that one. Just stares like, come on.

"What's your name?" Rebecca asks.

"Danielle."

"Did you know the sheriff's sister, Danielle?"

"Used to bike out here to get pie. Want to know more you could always ask the sheriff."

"I'm interested in your perspective."

"You know who knew her? Cassie Pennington. Go ask her."

"I'm asking you."

"Right, okay," Danielle says. "Cassie sorted mail at the post office until she was caught opening envelopes she wasn't supposed to. Got exiled back to the dirt farm for that. But while she was employed, she became friends with Dalise . . . uh, that's the sheriff's sister."

"I know."

"Dalise was always hanging around town to be near her brother, and I think Cassie talked to her on her lunch breaks."

"What mail did Cassie open?"

"Ask the mailmen. I think she's just touched in the head. My dad says she's crazier than an outhouse fly."

Rebecca thinks Danielle's dad understands the way things are around here.

"Anyone will tell you the sheriff's sister was young, and how it's a great shame, but there was no shortage of men who turned their heads to gawk as she passed by."

"Guys are something else," Rebecca says.

The young woman snorts, shakes her head as if it's the only way to change her expression.

"What'd they do to Dalise?"

"They killed her."

"I mean . . . what'd they do to her? In the barn."

"What'd you say your name was?"

"I didn't. It's Rebecca."

Danielle's eyes harden into little pellets of gravel. "Cut her from her skin. Hung it up in the barn like an old suit."

"Why did they do that?"

"Oh, the town loves to talk about why."

"Such as?"

"My hairdresser thinks Paul wanted to be a woman. How's that for starters? Others say Paul and Cassie were running drugs into town, killed the sheriff's sister to keep him complacent."

"Paul and Cassie," Rebecca says. "Were they that close?" Another surge of irrational anger mounts in her heart. Primal jealously she's never felt.

Danielle shrugs. "I couldn't say."

"Will Paul try and find Cassie? I mean, in your opinion."

"I don't believe Paul's alive."

"But if he is . . ."

"If he is, and that's a big if, I don't think much can keep those two apart."

"Peas in a pod?"

"Cassie's gonna snap one of these days. Kill people. And everyone will pretend they're surprised about it. A fortune teller would say it's already in the cards."

"You said the body of Dalise Cortez was found in your barn?"

Danielle points a finger. "Go right out that side door and you can see for yourself. Not sure what you're hoping to find, though."

"Me either," Rebecca says. "But I've come all this way."

"Knock yourself out."

"Thanks . . . this is a lot of pies."

"This is a business."

"Yeah, but . . . this is a lot."

"Some law against baking them?"

"I don't know any."

"Why do you care, then?"

"I just . . . noticed you already have a freezer full." Rebecca sails her thumb toward the freezer case. The frosted glass door brims with homemade meat pies among other things.

"Catered event," the woman says.

"Lucky them. They smell awesome."

"The best. Can I go, officer?"

"Oh, I'm not a cop."

"Could've fooled me." Danielle shrugs.

Rebecca watches her get back to work. She goes right into the kitchen and never comes out again.

15

THE BARN AWAITS REBECCA JUST through the side door.

She crosses a patch of ground where the gravel becomes dirt and then grass. The barn sits beside a feeding pen. Beyond it is a field of grazing sheep and clucking chickens.

Her phone buzzes in her pocket as soon as she steps inside. More desperation, just a bunch of would-be interruptions from a voice she doesn't care to hear. She swipes to ignore the conversation and figures Bret can keep shouting into traffic while she side-steps horse shit.

It's easy to find the spot where Dalise Cortez's skin was hung up. It's the only area in here where the walls are unnaturally bare.

"What were you going to do with this girl's skin, Paul?"

The sputtering reliability of a tractor grumbles up over the hill across the street. Rebecca turns and catches an older man eyeing her from atop a John Deere, chewing a cigar like it's beef jerky.

He drives right over and sits idling.

"You must be the Herbert in Herbert's Farm," she says.

He tries for a modest smile, but his face is all leather. "My farm, missy. You need help with the store then Danielle can take care of you."

Rebecca flashes the photo again. Thinks she might as well glue the damn thing to the palm of her hand. "Danielle thinks this guy's dead."

"She probably wishes it were so."

"You know him, then?"

"He used to screw his girlfriend right here inside these walls." Herbert frowns sour. "I can't tell you why. I look the sort of man who understands kids today? Probably looking for a thrill or some damn thing."

"You actually saw them?"

"Sure did. I've known Cassie Pennington since she spoke in baby coos. Recognized her right off. Probably wouldn't have known anything at all if not for the animals making ungodly noises out here at all hours of the night. To think what those sickos might've been doing to my—"

"Seriously? To your . . . horses?"

Herbert shrugs. "Anything's possible is what I'm saying. Some of these creatures ain't been right since. And I don't have it in my heart to know the truth. 'Cause then I might be tempted to load up the double barrel and . . . well, might not know it to look at me, but I am an animal lover at heart."

His face is harder than a leather switch, but his eyes are soft and Rebecca decides it's an easy thing to believe.

"To answer your question," he says. "No. I don't think he's dead."

"Why not?"

"Why would he be? Someone that foul ain't gonna do the world any favors by just up and disappearing. That'd be too easy on the rest of us. Nah. Someone that foul doesn't go quietly."

"That is what I'm afraid of," Rebecca says.

"Shoot straight with me, missy," Herbert says. "I like to know where a person stands on the things they're asking about. So, tell me . . . where are you on this?"

"I think he's here. Somewhere in town."

"And you're hunting him?" He smiles, finding comfort in that thought. "Knew it as soon as I glanced you from across the way."

"If I can ask . . . why is Danielle so sure that Paul is dead?"

Herbert frowns once more. His face looks most natural in that mode. "Danielle's world is here. Baking pies. Tending register. Feeding animals. She can pretend the world's frosted flakes and strawberries 'cause on these acres, that's exactly what it is. Is that boy dead? Not a chance in hell, missy. But she can afford to think it."

"Kids, right?"

The old man laughs. "We blame kids 'cause they're easy to blame. It's Bright Fork that's the problem. Place is changing."

"Changing?"

"City people moving here like there's a goddamn gold rush."

"Sick of the noise and the bustle and–"

"Made their corner of the world worse, then left in droves rather than fix it. Bringing there to here to do it all over again."

"What do the locals make of it?"

The farmer slaps his knee, makes some rusty hinge noise. "Driving up taxes? Driving out family businesses and then trying to bring in all their bullshit? We've had four town hall meetings so far just to keep goddamn Starbucks out of here. How do you think the locals are taking it?"

"Why Bright Fork, though?" Rebecca asks. "No offense. It's just that this place is–"

"In the middle of nowhere? That's why we like it. But them? Wish I knew."

"Another weird question," Rebecca says. "Do you do catering here?"

"Suppose we could if it ever came up. But it's never come up. Why?"

"No reason," she says. "Just think those pies in there look good and my mind went wandering."

"You want a pie, I'll get you a pie."

"No, really, it's okay."

But Herbert seems excited to get her one. Begins to climb down off the tractor, groaning and grumbling with every twitch of his muscles. To watch him struggle is devastating. Rebecca begs him to stop, but like every old man she's ever known, he's more stubborn than a house cat.

"It's fine," she says. "Really. I was just thinking out loud."

"Goddamn weather," he snaps, scapegoating the chilly air. "Ain't supposed to be this cold in spring." The old man hates it, but his aching body makes the concession easier than it should be. "Arthritis turns me tighter than a screw."

"Sorry to bother you," Rebecca says and starts to leave.

"Nothing to be sorry for," he says. "If you do find him . . . I hope you'll kill him."

"For the things he's done?"

"Aye, sure," the old man says. "But I'm talking about you."

"Me?"

"See it in your eyes. No offense, but you've already got one foot in the grave. I ain't one to pry, so I'm not gonna ask about it, but you got eyes like you're chasing Armageddon into a hurricane."

"Maybe I do," Rebecca says.

"I think about it, you know. Knowing those mad dogs were in my barn . . . so close to my daughter. Wind only needed to shift one way and they could've run across her and . . ." He doesn't finish that sentence.

"That's not going to happen," she says.

"Way I see it, you're looking for a righteous kill. You want the truth, I've laid in bed awake on more than one night wishing I'd blasted him with my double barrel."

Rebecca nods like she knows the feeling.

"I'm sorry to be so blunt about things, but I don't suffer fools gladly." Herbert clicks his tongue and offers a consolatory smile. "Truth of it anyway, I'm probably just exaggerating about that shotgun business."

"I wish you weren't," she says. "I wish you had done it."

16

HALFWAY BACK TO TOWN PROPER, Rebecca stomps the brakes.

Farmland stretches for miles on either side of the road, but something in the distance beyond the tilled earth catches her eye.

Her heart drums as she climbs out and hops the old log fence. The ancient wood wobbles beneath her weight and she curses like it's an obstacle placed here just to slow her down.

At the back of the field and facing the forest stands an army of scarecrows. Spaced perfectly like infantrymen on a battlefield.

Rebecca strides toward them, counting the sprawl of bodies as she goes.

Fourteen in total.

None are as sharp-dressed as the sentry hoisted up at the Pennington Residence. These wear shredded denim and torn plaid. Homemade straw hats. No animal heads here. Just button eyes sewn on stained burlap. Rebecca goes all the way down the line, inspecting each like a drill instructor.

Why would anyone place this many together?

A few of the scarecrows have shirt flaps undone. Rebecca reaches up and pulls the fabric aside. Bloodstained hay bales are stuffed hastily inside the recessed cavity. She lifts the flap higher and finds the area around the hole is rotted flesh that's wet, on the verge of liquefaction. Small, emaciated breasts dangle off worn skin that's tight against rounded ribs.

Rebecca gasps, fingers to mouth, as she steps back and looks down the line. She half expects all the burlap heads to be craned in her direction and is relieved when they're not. She moves to the next scarecrow and finds the same arrangement beneath its shirt. Raisin breasts, gray skin. Long dead. Checks another. Keeps going until she's got fourteen hay-stuffed corpses, each of them female. Their clothes are torn at random where birds have pecked little hunks of meat off their bones, and she doesn't have to examine those holes any further to know that flies have long since laid eggs inside of them. If Rebecca listens close, she can almost hear the maggots crunching their way through flesh, breaking these bodies down to nothing.

"He hasn't stopped," she says, almost silent. Paul hasn't stopped committing murders at all. He's only getting started.

Rebecca can't speak to anyone about this. A decision that's antithetical to a quarter-century of sharply honed law enforcement instincts. Blowing the whistle on these bodies means Bright Fork gets more attention–probably federal. Washington's about as smart as a stick, but there's nowhere to hide in a town this small. Sooner or later she'd be tripping over feds.

And if Special Agent Dale Cooper does come to town, Paul will know right off who he's looking for. If Paul disappears again, Rebecca will never find him.

That's not an option.

She stares up at the fourteen bodies, all mothers and daughters, wondering how in the hell so many people can go missing without a whisper?

You know why, she thinks. It's not even really a question.

"Paul isn't the only one."

17

ST. CECILIA'S SITS AT THE OTHER edge of town, surrounded by forests so thick it seems to Rebecca she's traveled back in time.

She rolls to a stop at the tip of the narrow path where the road bottlenecks, flanked by tombstones so old their engravings have been smoothed away. Completely erased. This country isn't as old as these markers look.

Her head throbs. Only a few pills rattle around inside the Advil bottle now.

A young priest in a gray frock appears in the doorway. He smiles guiltily. Behind him, the thick oak slams shut, sending the perched ravens overhead scattering.

"Not many visitors out here," he says. The meaning behind his words is, Why are you here?

"Not visiting." Rebecca fishes for the Advil and eyes the father through the windshield. He stuffs a tease of tobacco inside his corn-cob pipe, settles against a tree.

Rebecca decides she might need her pistol, too, forgetting for a moment Cortez is holding onto it for safekeeping.

"What are you selling, then?" he says as she climbs out.

"Sightseeing."

With a grin, "Well, why didn't you say so?"

"You taking over this parish?"

He *tsks* his tongue, suddenly sad in a way that wouldn't fool a voter. "I am," he says, then adds "regrettably" before pouting his lips. His mouth is the size of a bullhorn, and his receding hairline's half-way gone. "Helping the world to move on from such an . . . unspeakable tragedy. Father Kindry was beloved."

She starts past and he sticks his arm out. He doesn't touch, only signals a stop as he lifts his chin to get a better look at this sightseer. The smoke rising up from his pipe becomes a veil between them.

Rebecca holds there a quick moment. For a second, there's something familiar about him. A face you met at a dinner party long ago, with whom you exchanged brief pleasantries. A face she's dreamt. But, no, this is a stranger's face and anything more is just a trick of the light . . . right? Rebecca looks him over again, decides, yes.

"Okay," he says. Repeats "Okay" and laughs about it. "It is hardly our custom to scrutinize. God's house is open to any and all." He lifts his arm like it's a tollbooth gate and Rebecca heads toward the narthex.

Old habits strike Rebecca there. Alien gestures that belong to the world she left behind. The urge to sign the cross upon entrance. She's close to doing it, fingers gliding toward the holy water bowl. She stops just as they're about to take the dip and thinks, Nope.

That life's gone. The man upstairs doesn't want her now. Because she'd never be able to look at him and repent for the things she's done.

For what she's about to do.

Her Uggs sound like horse clops as she walks the center aisle. At first glance, it's any old church. Funded by the local diocese, but living mainly off whatever the people of Bright Fork can afford to donate. Not very showy. Stain glass windows throw kaleidoscopic shadows across the floor and rainbow light shimmers in her peripheral.

The priest comes back inside while she's lost in prosaic thoughts—

weddings, first communions, hers and Jaime's, all the lies she used to tell herself about the lord's grand designs.

The priest stands inside the narthex. His hand rakes the wall of pamphlet literature while tobacco notes spread the smell of roasted leaves. The way the window light catches him only a few jagged slats of his face are visible, revealing wide-flung Bela Lugosi eyes.

"Tell me about this site," Rebecca says suddenly, almost unconsciously.

He stands unmoving. Rebecca resumes her stroll, loud footsteps circling the nave as she examines the altar from afar.

"Site," he says as if he needed extra time to conjure the right amount of indignant.

"Yeah."

"Seems you already know something."

"I know we love to pretend that Christianity was the first practiced religion in the United States." Rebecca's heart rate quickens at the challenge. This is a heated conversation now and she doesn't know why. Only that her opinions on this are absolute.

"Oh, I'm sure there were others . . . but what matters is—"

"Whether it's Protestantism, Catholicism, doesn't especially matter. Because what they don't tell you is many of these churches were built where they are very deliberately."

"Deliberately?" he speaks with insufferable smugness.

"To cover up pagan sites from one coast to the next," Rebecca says. These words are hers, birthed from knowledge that is not. The blood coursing through her veins suddenly hurts, as if thickened jelly is being pumped to her organs.

"Pagan sites." He's got a leaflet in his hands now—*On the importance of baptizing your child in Christ*—crumples it. Tosses it atop the small table of candles where it catches fire, withering and burning into a blackened claw.

"Vatican's way of rewriting history," Rebecca says. "Erect sacred and protected sites on grounds that were here long before."

"You sound so certain of this, it would almost be impolite of me to challenge you." His face teems with a smile he can barely hold back.

"It's pretty clever, you ask me." Rebecca's fingertips tingle. The fillings in her back molars dance. She scratches her scalp and tears two strips of flesh away like wet tissue. In the dark space between her blinking eyes, the red-faced woman stares back, mouth propped wide in a silent scream.

It's like looking into a funhouse mirror and snatching the very worst memory of yourself from twenty-five years ago.

The priest comes from the shadows, seemingly electrified. He points at Rebecca like he suddenly recognizes her. "You feel it."

Rebecca reaches for the photo, starts to ask. The priest waves it away. He has no interest in looking. This conversation's beyond that. He starts to laugh fondly at the sight of her, but the tobacco has blunted his voice so it sounds more like he's clearing his throat.

She spins in the center aisle and notices at last why this place feels so inherently wrong. It's the only Catholic Church she's ever seen that's entirely devoid of Christian iconography. No Stations of the Cross, no hymn books in the pews, and nothing at all to indicate Messianic identity.

Windows and murals showcase rustic landscapes and cracking skies. Heavy rain pelts kneeling peasants. A field of stone markers stands unmolested. A crowd huddled together around a fire, pointing in horror at an elongated silhouette emerging from the dark of the forest. Everything here is old world European. Pagan. And the longer she looks, the emptier she feels.

Above the altar, a mass of sculpted ceramic hangs suspended. It's not Christ on the cross, but something harder to describe. A torso. Humanoid in shape, with stylized gray flesh that kind of resembles the protective exterior of a hornet's nest—chaotic patterns rushing everywhere and folding beneath themselves. On the sculpture's shoulders sits a flat-topped head. The kind of nest you'd find in the gutter of an abandoned barn—even more swollen and delineated than the body. This "face" is without features, save for the oval entry hole positioned in the precise spot where a mouth would be.

This perfect blank, with that awful, swirling mouth pitched in disbelief, looks down on Rebecca in somber judgment. That she has its attention at all makes the warmth inside her flicker like a candle in a blizzard.

"Go on." The priest stands behind her now. Sour breath gusts across her neck. Spit crackles and pops in her ear as he licks his lips in anticipation. She feels his hands hovering over her shoulders, down her arms, around her hips . . .

Never touching, but always close.

It's the prod she needs. Rebecca passes beneath the sculpture to ascend thick marble steps. Echoes like wishing well screams. An opened book sits atop the altar cloth. The words are in English, but as soon as she reads them, they begin to animate and swirl and her eyes feel dizzy watching the text become an inky blur.

Then the world follows suit.

Outside the windows, the sun sets in fast-forward. Crickets chirp in high-pitched squeaks. The pages rearrange into symbols she can no longer read.

Rebecca's eyes roll back into her head, finding darkness first and then the young red face waiting there. Green eyes roll down and put color inside the strange girl's cloud-white orbs.

"Read it." Her voice is a muffled, underwater gargle.

"You heard it, didn't you?" The priest grins, suddenly standing against Rebecca's face. He's eager to know, but keeps just enough distance, as if locked into place by an invisible leash. His eyes continue to widen and he looks desperate. Can't look away.

Neither can she.

The rising sun scales the sky and beams through the windows once more. The priest is caught there, and the light renders his skin translucent. His flesh looks like a plastic bag stretched tight around contents ready to burst through. What's beneath this façade is inhuman, and she can no longer stand the sight. Beady, briquette eyes. A mouth so wide its thin lips seem to stretch off the sides of its fake human face.

This realization prompts Rebecca to retreat. She starts down the far aisle when she blinks and glimpses the red face again.

Each blink summons more than just that face. Rebecca hears her voice each time her eyes fall.

"It's . . ."

Blink.

". . . not . . ."

Blink.

". . . yours . . ."

Blink.

". . . to read."

At that, Rebecca squeezes her eyes shut and finds the face staring straight through her. Can't focus on anything beyond the blood. It's just slathered everywhere. More than just a face, there's a body, too. Cold hands spring outward and seize Rebecca's wrists with searing frostbite.

"It's mine."

When Rebecca opens her eyes, she's alone in the church. Each window is flanked with the Stations of the Cross that weren't there before. And there's no priest here, she knows, because her thrill killers slaughtered him like an animal. Hanging over her head is a sculpture of Jesus Christ.

She mumbles those very words beneath her breath, presses the book tight against her chest and rushes out.

18

REBECCA DRIVES TO THE CENTER of town because she's shaken up and needs to be around whatever passes for normal in Bright Fork. Sits on the hood of her car across from the park and tries to enjoy the fresh air. Clearing her head's impossible, but every so often she remembers what peace of mind feels like.

The air is chilled and the occasional gust refreshes her all the way down to her pores. She unbuttons the first few of her blouse to expose as much of her flesh as decency allows.

The park isn't much to look at. An empty gazebo sits dead center surrounded by well-kept flowerbeds. A few of the trees have plaques at the bases, in memory of the town's founding fathers. The place is nearly deserted, save for one mother pushing a baby stroller along the far edge of the grass, away from town center.

The book sits in Rebecca's lap. A few minutes ago, it had been some generic hardcover thing you'd find in any church across America. Now, the cover's old. Sunken intaglio print engraved in the lines. Written in a language long lost and forever secret is the title Rebecca can suddenly read.

On The Decretals Of Tanner Red

She pages through. Text is wrapped around crude illustrations of cruder sexual acts. Young and petite female bodies violated by a shape that in no way resembles anything human, though the meaning is clear–she's seeing Tanner Red.

The pages are thick. The acids on her fingertips stain with blasphemous curiosity. The last nine pages are of different paper stock, thinner and cheaper and appear to have been added much later, part of the binding carefully removed in order to squeeze them in before reattaching it. The book feels overstuffed and slightly awkward as a result.

Her hand leafs through, trawling illustrated and forbidden rituals. Part of her admires these. Superstitions kept the world docile and controllable, and if the followers of Tanner Red lived up to even a fraction of what He asks here, they'd have done some real living that she hasn't.

Rebecca chases that envy off as she thumbs back to those last nine pages and begins to read. And then reread. Tears nest around her eyes and for some reason, she thinks, Finally.

Rebecca wonders why the priest allowed her to take the book out of there but figures it's obvious enough.

He wants me to see this.

The final nine pages begin with a brief description of the travelers who landed on the shores of this New World–these people, The First, were ostracized for their denial of Christianity and believed they'd find seclusion in these unnamed wilds of future America.

They establish temporary shelters, raid the enveloping forests for whatever sustenance can be sacked away against the incoming cold. And yet, it's not enough to merely survive. They came to find fulfillment without persecution. They came for Him. They go to work on the most important task of all–summoning.

It's months before they can.

They need the rebirth, but winter is long. Uncertain. Worry is scratched into their faces during the seemingly eternal night. Still, they practice tribute. Coupling bodies by firelight in large groups or in traded partners. There is no monogamy here.

The thaw comes and preparations begin. The ritual is ready for fallow ground: A mass of moans and orgasms that ignite the air. Spilt seed sows the earth and the two in combination create the sounds and smells that lure Him forth from the abyss.

In those woods, in the place deemed by The First as the Village of Gar, the one they call Tanner Red moves between worlds.

They see him just beyond the dark of the forest. Pacing the clearing like a long-caged beast. Drawing off the energy of the tribute. A body attuning once more to its motions.

The eldest villager walks out reluctantly to greet Him, torch in hand, raised high to the night.

She's never seen again. It barely matters.

This land of Gar was theirs.

It's now His.

The sick return to health. The earth is easier to till. Every crop is beyond bountiful.

In the woods surrounding them, native tribes begin to compete for scavenge. They strike at night, dealing heavy bloodshed. In order to keep hunting and gathering, The First asks Him for protection.

Offerings such as this are never made lightly, but considering Gar's dwindling resources, the natives may win the war.

This is desperation. And desperation breeds sacrifice.

So it's a lottery. The village gathers for evening commune, thanks and praise, and the patron who discovers a swab of red paint on the underside of their plate is to be the chosen one.

Tanner Red is aroused by such placation. Grows accustomed to the flesh as a result of this sacrifice. He begins whispering to the women of Gar on evening winds. They soon succumb to the idea of lying with a god–privilege too great to resist. As the men go off to battle once more, He comes.

The skies over Gar thrum with ecstatic cries that explode the valley.

The men return and discover bulging stomachs the size of boulders. Children are born from every able womb in just a few short weeks.

The men are cruel. They attempt to force confessions from their partners and lovers. No matter how hard they beat, the stories are the same.

The men are angry. They stay in Gar long enough to dress their wounds and heal. Then set off to hunt the god they had summoned to protect them.

One season passes. Then another. They never return.

To the women of Gar, this matters little. Each is too busy raising their blessed child. And He provides all that's necessary in the ways of sustenance and fortune. Lean winters, ample crops, complete self-sufficiency.

In time, the children learn the practices of men.

In time, others from the Old World come and discover Gar.

In time, Tanner Red spreads like a fever to other colonies.

But in the minds of the oldest, there remains the action of a merciless god. One who takes what He wants and who spares none from humiliation.

He senses this resentment and chooses to act through the men, instead of on behalf of them. The seeds of husbands and lovers form the life spark this time. And the world is good again.

So good that other religions begin surfacing inside Gar. Some of these faiths do not demand as much from their followers.

But creatures of pride do not fare well when deprived of worship. The unbelievers in Gar are stricken with illness. The curse spreads further, striking out at committed followers should they bother to treat those already suffering.

The women turn barren. Worse, their innards become shriveled and diseased. They begin to rot from the inside out. Clustered pustules line their bladders and intestines, spilling from their holes in sickly, runny globs of yellow. Their cunts drip with rot, the same poison seeping from their mouths, a stench so putrid even animals refuse to venture anywhere near Gar.

It's the women this time who tire of their god's cruelty. Only a devil would turn their bodies against them. They will go out into the world, not with weapons but with their bodies, and confront the thing called Tanner Red in a way He will not resist.

They trek to the Barrens, to the place of their first ritual and cast off their clothing, squatting onto the ring of stone phalluses they've stuffed down inside the ground. They force their broken and diseased bodies to perform tribute, done solely in defiance.

He is unmoved, but too vain to acknowledge this as anything but desperate apologia.

But they have figured out how to revoke His domain. And on this spot, deemed this day The Plowing Fields, the women of Gar assert their freedom. And to their surprise, they see Him once more in the woods. A rough-skinned figure without features, one humbled hand reaching outward, one final plea for mercy as hunks of His body crack and crumble and then blow through the air like scattering ash.

Their denial drives Him back beneath the earth. Into the world between worlds.

Nothing of Him will be remembered. Unlike the men whose might and muscle led them to extinction, the women return home victorious and decree their current way of life be destroyed.

Tanner Red's most loyal followers are slain that night.

The women, too diseased to live among the world, embrace finality in the wilderness. The healthy are brought into neighboring communities where they are encouraged to forget about the gospel of flesh and instead adopt another, more caring faith.

The women sleep more soundly in their new lives, but as birthrates decline due to elements and diseases, there remains temptation for the old way. Only it's buried now and He does not seem to have a way back.

Except that He does . . .

The rest of these amended pages, however many there originally were, are torn out.

Rebecca's stomach twists into knots as she reaches the end of the book once more. She's sick of reading it and slams it shut. As sickened as she is, her fingers stoke the cover with curiosity. Maybe even admiration.

It's gotten late. Rebecca is ready to call it a day when she looks up to stretch her eyes and is unable to reconcile the terrain sprawled before her. The gazebo and surrounding landscape are gone, traded for a circle of knee-high statues sitting way down there—at the end of a long walk.

She starts down to where the earth is dirt and thinks what she sees is stone carved flowers planted in an otherwise fallow garden.

Downtown Bright Fork is nowhere to be seen, just empty grass-lands—earth that squishes around her feet.

The moon hovers behind a scratch of gray clouds that lift like a curtain, casting the ground there in a natural spotlight.

The fates wish for Rebecca to see the truth. She walks toward the circle of statues, catching rising bile that fills her throat like a flooded basement. She knows what she's looking at because the book clutched beneath her arm has told her.

Deep-rooted stone phalluses, twelve of them, form a circle. The Plowing Fields. She reaches out to touch one. Not in admiration, but because she has always believed her eyes. Until lately.

The stone is smooth to touch. Shafts are thin enough for her fingers to get around. Each one of these is capped by a wider head.

And without understanding what's happening, she steps away and keeps stepping, afraid to turn her back for fear of this terrible thing disappearing. Because if it does, she can no longer trust herself at all. She moves back up the incline without ever once taking her eyes off the display, praying it stays right there.

19

THE HEADACHE STRIKES MID-GAIT. THIS one's unlike the others.

The world dials to white and shanks her equilibrium. Rebecca sails horizontal and skids through the muck like she's diving for home.

She looks up, the usual blown-out white fades away in the aftermath until there's focus. She realizes she's staring up at the sun and a ring of silhouetted townies circling overhead. For the second time in as many goddamn days.

"You again?"

"What's her problem?"

"Drugs."

"Don't you know all the girls today take cocaine?"

"Always in a hurry, too."

Not a single one of them helps her up. That's good. Rebecca would rather everyone in this place keep their fucking hands off. She lifts herself and rolls onto her back, sits up and barks for space.

Bright Fork has returned in full. The gazebo and its surrounding flowers are there in the distance. The Plowing Fields are a dream that's nowhere to be seen.

Rebecca stands hobbled and limps the few feet to her car.

"Miss . . ."

She isn't going to turn because she has nothing to say to anyone. Opens the door and a hand taps her back.

A girl with jet-black hair and movie star eyes has dislodged from the crowd and flashes a confident smile. "Don't forget your bible." She holds it out like it's steaming garbage. Rebecca snatches it back and mumbles a humiliated thank you. The girl gets back in line, sipping some awful green drink out of a small to go cup while staring at Rebecca like she's a zoo animal.

Rebecca can't get out of there fast enough. She twists the ignition and speeds off down the road toward the motel.

"Of course," she grouses as she finds Cortez waiting for her in the parking lot. He laughs at the sight of her. His might be the only friendly face in town, but she doesn't want the company. Company complicates things.

"People love to talk about you," he says.

"People should find something else to worry about."

"Crazy woman passing out every day in public—"

"What do they do?" she asks. "Text you real time updates? It literally just happened."

"Got two calls on you the moment it did," he says. "Already a pool down at Martin's Pub on where in town you'll fall tomorrow. Put $20 on the library steps myself."

"Hardy har har. I didn't pass out. I tripped."

"Yeah, that's what it looks like."

"Okay," she growls. "Have a good night, Sheriff."

"Here's the thing I need . . ." Cortez looks like he knows he ain't supposed to ask, but isn't going to let that stop him. He stares at Rebecca like she's the only one who's got the answer. "Tell me how you keep going."

"Coffee."

"Not what I mean."

"I can't—"

"Please," he says. "I see it in your eyes. You've got that same parasite sucking on your soul. People here ask for help and I can't bring myself to care anymore. About anything. I want blood and that's not who I am. Last night, I considered eating a bullet . . . I can see that dance with death in your eyes, too."

"I'm not your priest," Rebecca says. "Don't look at me like I can save your soul."

How can he ask this, given what she's here to do? What he knows she's going to do. His drooping eyes make him look like a whipped dog. He's desperate to shake the pain. And desperate people look anywhere for salvation, even at a devil.

Turns out, "Nothing" is the answer Cortez expects. His head tilts down as he thinks it over. Once he realizes Rebecca's giving him snake eyes, he starts off without another word.

Rebecca watches him go, but only because she can't bring herself to move. His question has resurrected that night. The night when all the pain and grief wrecked her life all the way down to the foundation.

She remembers the last few precious seconds of it, hurrying from the laundry room with a basket of Bret's work clothes fresh from the dryer as her phone beeped and barked from the couch, preparing to deliver the three simple words that would end it all in the blink of an eye.

Your daughter's dead.

Now Rebecca is thinking about everything. The last two years come clawing at the door like a freezing animal. The immeasurable grief. The quickness with which she set aside her mourning, her mind settling for endless revenge fantasies.

It's terrifying how fast that happens. You just know it's over. The things you have are as good as gone. And the relationships you've fed are about to starve.

Nothing gets out unscathed.

Rebecca remembers sleeping on her side because she hates the stupid look engrained on Bret's face. All those frumpy "why can't you get over it" looks that eventually morphed his features into permanent disgust. Sex suddenly becomes a repulsive thought. The physical act is nothing to her, and when she tries it in order to appease her husband's "needs" she nearly freaks out because she can no longer stand for him to touch her like that.

Bret thinks she's gone too far off the deep end. Thinks she needs a shrink. Sure. She goes. Because she can't focus enough to work. She cooperates but has no intention of getting to the root of it all. Paul's the root. And he needs to be extracted. Bret begs her to get help. Finds a little clinic in Vermont that's supposed to be very good.

Bret's excited.

Rebecca pretends to be.

But therapy there is all salient nods and "picture blue skies." Forgetting is murder. Treatment means killing the only thing she's got left. Her pain. The drugs scramble her skull like eggs, ripping thoughts away with alarming precision. Worst part of it is that they don't work the way they're supposed to.

She never forgets about Paul.

Probably because she never wants to.

And that's the thing about Sheriff Cortez. The thing she doesn't have the heart to say to him or to anyone else whose life has been damaged by premature loss. He's desperate for a way back. Everyone stands on that precipice. A choice needs to be made, like taking an exit off the highway. Miss it and there's no backing up. Miss it and your picket fences and fresh-cut grass get broken and dead.

So how do you keep going, Sheriff? Rebecca thinks. You just go. Go until you're even. Not a split second after that matters worth a damn.

Cortez is nearly to his car when he turns and starts back, shaking his head as he comes. "I'm off for the night," he says. "Doing a taco run. Want to get dinner with me? They won't even care you're dressed like that."

Rebecca shakes her head. No, not tonight. Not ever. She's hardly worth the niceties.

"Please," he says. "You're the only one I can talk to."

All she can do is shake like a bobble toy. It's just easier than articulating. He opens his mouth to press the issue and she rolls her eyes–here it comes–then hopes Cortez has missed the gesture. She doesn't want to hurt him.

"I've got work to do," she says. Holds the book and waves it around, and then as if remembering the world had practiced civility before moving on, she flashes an empty smile and says, "Thank you for thinking of me." People like the sheriff are good, and what little good remains in this place should be nurtured.

"Thinking of you is all I do," he says. But that comes out wrong. Maybe. Rebecca recoils, feels her expression fall because forget poker faces when all you're looking to do is put one sick bastard out of his misery.

The sheriff stammers, sensing he's blown his shot at evening company. He still coasts back up to Rebecca, who stands and watches, feeling nothing but pity for this man.

"What I meant is . . . I'm rooting for you to make sense of this. For–"

"I know," Rebecca says. "Trust me, Sheriff. I want my gun back."

A smile at the corners of his mouth. He shuffles closer, glances around like a nervous schoolyard boy. She wonders how old he is and doesn't think he's even forty. "What have you got there?" His fingers brush the book.

Oh no, she thinks. I wouldn't know where to begin. "Too early to tell."

"Maybe I can–"

"No, no," she says. "I work alone. If it points to anything, I'll let you know. Okay?"

Cortez nods slowly. He realizes it's as good a deal as he's going to get. "Hey, tell you what . . . i'll bring you back a couple of tacos and you can brief me on what you've got. How's that sound?"

Christ, it sounds awful, but this guy could put her on the hook if he wants. And so far he's done exactly the opposite. "Sure," she says.

"Great, it'll take some time, I've got an errand to run and some rounds to make."

"I'll watch for you in the window."

Cortez laughs, points toward her room and offers to walk her up. They go in silence, him trailing a few steps behind and mostly glancing at the ground. They pause beneath the warm glow of the yellow wall sconce. Now he looks her over like something's wrong.

"Yeah," she says. "I know. I've got mud all over me."

"Ain't that." He gets closer and for a second she thinks he's going to try and force a kiss. Braces herself and balls her fingers into a fist. "You got two different color eyes," he says.

"What?" She doesn't think anyone's ever studied her face this hard, not even Bret, and suddenly she's compelled to turn her head this way and that, up and down, letting him study all the angles. "Gotta be a trick of the light."

"It's not," he says. "Yesterday your eyes were brown. Today that one's green." He points to her right one.

"I-I don't understand what's happening to me." She unlocks her room and starts in.

"Check yourself out you don't believe me," Cortez says. "You got a mirror in there?"

"I've got two." She disappears into the darkness, leaving the sheriff to watch the door slam on his face.

20

REBECCA SITS CROSS-LEGGED ON THE bed, her clothes in a muddy ball at her feet. Bret is busy feeding another string of texts through the phone. She barely acknowledges them. The book rests in her lap.

She flips toward the earliest pages while around her the mirrors make predictable hell. These are raucous knocks—they've never been this loud or this agitated, going well beyond fingernail taps on glass. These are the sounds of rounded fists falling and falling and falling.

Because they want to get in.

But human beings are nothing if not adaptable. People teach themselves to live with all kinds of setbacks: limp legs, ringing ears, or lumps beneath their arms. Anything to avoid going to the doctor. Inconvenience is a sliding scale that tips surprisingly far when it needs to. And Rebecca has decided she'll go the rest of her life without ever seeing her reflection again.

"Is that the best you can do?" she taunts, elbowing the wall. Her headache is especially sharp tonight. It makes her irritable. Those hands don't care. They continue to pound as if on instinct.

"Where's my fucking Advil?" Rebecca says. This pain has laid eggs inside her brain. She feels as though she's dealing with a hundred hatchlings at once. Mini migraines crawl into every crevice of her skull, wreaking havoc on her thoughts and keeping her temples pulsing. Her eyes, watery.

She finds the bottle of Advil on the desk, opened and knocked aside. Empty. Can't even remember how many she's taken today. Recalls her doctor cautioning against liver damage and the way she laughed in his face.

"Screw it," she says. She'll push on. The weathered page between her fingers feels culled from another world. Old and faded sketches show undocumented history. She flips further back and realizes the text is all symbols.

Somehow she understands it.

You know why, she thinks.

"I do?" she says.

She does.

Rebecca picks up her phone, sighs as she sees herself in low light. It's not the same as looking at oneself in the mirror. The knocks don't come through here. She looks slightly out of focus and no matter which way she turns her head, just looks damn old. Every angle, an unflattering one.

She stares straight into the screen and clicks the button. Has to zoom in close in order to see it, but Cortez was right. One of her eyes is the color of jade. But it's even worse than that. The entire shape of that eye is different and now that she's scrutinizing, she realizes it's altered the structure of her face.

This is a stranger's face. Parts of it still belong to her, but continued scrutiny makes her headache grow.

She throws the phone down and slips into sweat pants and a loose top, walks down to the office—glad to leave the sound of knocking mirrors behind.

"The hell do you want?" the manager says as she steps inside. He looks up from a Hungry Man and has brownie crumbs plastered to his chin. She doesn't have a chance to respond before he picks himself up out of his recliner. "Last time. Hear me?"

They foot it back up to Paul's room, except he's all the more pissed off about it this time, giving her a look that asks, "How many times are you going to make me do this?"

At least the mirrors in here are shattered.

She tried that once herself. On the night she fled the hospital. Wrapped her fist inside the thick padding of a bloody straightjacket and sent knuckles sailing straight on. Her fist smashed glass, but her forearm kept going. Straight into water darker than night and thicker than oil.

It's the kind of thing that conveniently happens to people in loony bins. That way, doctors can talk about you in hushed tones as they scribble notes and shake their heads because you're an A-number-1 tragedy.

The shit-smeared symbols decorating this room feel more familiar now that she's read the book. Paul used the old-world alphabet in those pages to spell words in here.

Spell them in shit.

She sits on the floor and opens the book. Pages through. Looks for runes that match Paul's fecal penmanship.

"There we go," she says.

The first one might say INVITATION. The second could read HARVEST. The third's probably REBIRTH. There's a certain rationale to that based on the history she's read. But the fourth scrawl, above the busted television, remains completely illegible.

"You're in here somewhere," Rebecca says, flipping the pages. Close enough to feel the truth in her fingertips. One page shows a gnarled hand reaching out from a darkened forest. Fingers about to close around the throat of a virginal girl. It would be a basic illustration if not for the incredible detail in the child's face, pained eyes, and hypocritically pursed lips.

This illustration is THE VEIL.

Then there's the ash on the bathroom floor. Paul has burnt the truth to prevent anyone else from following him *on ahead for Tanner Red.*

Her fingers stroke the jagged tears in the back of the book and she smiles as a piece of the puzzle clicks into place.

"Where'd you go, Paul?"

Rebecca rushes back to her room. Even in the chilly night, she's getting too hot beneath the collar. Strips her clothes off as soon as she's in.

The shades are drawn tight and Rebecca stretches on the bed, listening to the mirror knocks. Suddenly, there's competing bustle in the parking lot. She peeks out behind the slat and watches as the spaces fill up with cars. Bodies shuffle to their rooms.

It's three in the morning. Every vacancy is filled within the hour.

Rebecca eyes the Wild Turkey on the desk. Her underarms are slick from moisture. It's a steady 68 in here. Sweat beads at her hairline. She wipes it with her underwear.

Bourbon's poison but she's going to take it. Blacking out is maybe the only way to sleep without seeing that face. Without suffering someone else's memories. Last thing she wants to do is call Bret in the morning and navigate an entire conversation of *why haven't you called me back* when all she needs to know is was there ever a time when we stole a classic Volkswagen Beetle and went joyriding up to York Beach?

For the record, Bret had said there wasn't.

The bottleneck goes to her lips. During her first swallow, Rebecca thinks about how much she wants to die.

She curls on the floor with the bottle in her fist, blinks and finds the red face standing in the darkness in the far-off distance.

Blink.

The young girl wears tight blue jeans. A tighter halter-top with cat whiskers stretched across her breasts. Blond hair in a ponytail.

Rebecca remembers buying that outfit.

Another swig, then another. And one more for good measure. Anything to forget.

Blink.

The girl's closer. The tapping glass gets more agitated as she nears.

Blink.

Rebecca takes a swig so deep it's half the bottle.

Blink.

Her thoughts blur.

Red-stained eyelids lift to reveal jade eyes beneath. Neon green emanates like a snapped glow stick, igniting the contours of this mangled face. Rebecca remembers how bright these eyes once beamed. She remembers rocking them to sleep and wondering what the future meant. Remembers the pride they had when it came time to glue a macaroni mane on top of a lion drawing. Green eyes brighter than summer grass, now muted and cool–the world after a thunderstorm.

"Hi, Mom," Jaime says.

Rebecca tries to get the bottle to her lips, but it's too late. Still, she tries. She's willing to take down the rest in a single gulp if that's what it's going to take to exorcise this perversity from her skull.

Though Jaime would rather she not.

The headache returns and Rebecca can barely see from behind waterlogged eyes. Her neck stretches like elastic and her spine does little chiropractic cracks to accommodate the growth. What little breath she can get through her nose comes with heavy sniffles. She opens her mouth to scream and four fingertips appear beneath her upper lip. A wiggling thumb scrapes the inside of her cheek as it snaps to freedom, flexing in the cool air.

A whole wrist slides from Rebecca's mouth.

The mirrors are riled. An army of inquisitive hands knocks beyond them now.

Rebecca doubles over. The hand pushes from her mouth and reaches to the floor, trying to force Rebecca's body back upright. The pain's a snakebite twisting her throat and stomach around as the invading presence mounts its escape. She feels her innards sloshing and the tightening in her body is as bad as giving birth–if you had to push a baby through your throat.

The hand is free all the way up to its forearm, waving through the air and eager to grip something in order to pull the rest of the body free. Another hand scales the inside of her ribcage, climbing it like a ladder.

Rebecca thinks she's going to die.

She flails. The Wild Turkey spills. She reaches for something. Anything she can get her hands on. Any way to end her suffering. If she's not already in hell then she's certainly en route.

Whatever's happening terrifies her. She wishes she hadn't chased Cortez off. Jesus, even in this unexplainable moment she cannot believe how scared she is of being alone. She wobbles close to the full mirror and thinks if this is the way she has to go, then she's ready to yank that fucking sheet away and make this stop.

No, Jaime screams inside her head. Do not do this.

And then . . . Jaime says nothing more.

The arm recedes back into Rebecca's mouth, as if a simple breath is enough to suck it all the way back down to wherever the hell it lives. There's relief. She's slicked with more sweat than a sauna and at last she can breathe again.

Rebecca's spasms have brought her a little too close to the glass. Her knees pop as she stands, hands on thighs as she finds her breath. Takes a seat on the bed and rubs her temples, feeling like her eyeballs need to be pushed back inside her skull before she can even begin to collect her–

The mirror bends like rubber. A projectile stretches out with the bed comforter dangling off it like a spearhead. Beneath the fabric, the outline is pointed fingers. They move like a missile straight for her. Rebecca crab-walks up against the headboard, palm pressed against her mouth to stifle the horrible scream that rubs her lungs raw.

The arm extends as far as it can go. The glass creaks like bending wood as the wiggling fingers reach in desperation, unable to get all the way to her throat. Whatever's beneath the sheet begins to regress back toward the frame. Rebecca watches it fall away, restoring first the rippling glass and then the comforter that blots it.

It's quiet for a long time then. Only Rebecca's sniffles punctuate the silence. The red face has gone into hiding now that she wants desperately to see it. Rebecca's got a million questions, but the only one she really wants to ask is, "Are you all right?"

She thinks of calling Bret, but what would he say? That she needs to get back to therapy yesterday. And that's not what this is. This is a chance to put things right.

A chance for the Daniels Family to be whole again.

Rebecca sobs into her hands. Two years' worth of pent up tears slicking her palms. For the first time in what feels to her like forever, there's nothing to be sad about.

These are tears of joy.

21

"JAIME," REBECCA SAYS INTO THE air.

She sits on the bed calling for her daughter the way you summon the family dog. She slaps her thigh over and over and gets only silence.

It's still 68 in here, but she's cooking.

Rebecca goes to the shower, hopping from bed-to-bed in order to keep away from the mirror.

In the bathroom she cranks the knob all the way hot and hugs the far wall to distance herself from the medicine cabinet glass. The sweatshirt she's got fastened to it is holding up well so far.

The piping stream reddens her skin like a boiled lobster, but the need to scrub mud and grime from her body supersedes the civil war raging in her mind.

"Jaime," she repeats. "Please come back. Don't be afraid that I know it's you."

Jaime has nothing to say.

"Why didn't you ask for help?" Rebecca says. "I'm going to find him, you know. I'm going to find Paul and, well . . ." It still feels weird to say it out loud—another habit from the old world. Her oath to protect and to serve feels laughably antiquated now.

The girl is still here, though. Still inside. The way her heart pumps hard. The presence of those swirling memory fragments. Jaime's memories. And there's the way her body chemistry surges on promises of murder.

"Is that what you want?" Rebecca asks. She shuts her eyes and buries her head against her forearm, trying to will the red face from hiding. "It's the only thing I've wanted since . . ."

Jaime is there. In the darkness, bloodstained fingers reach out.

And as soon as they do, the tapping resumes on the other side of the drawn shower curtain. Muffled clinks underneath that sweatshirt. Slow at first, but ramping up fast. Growing more restless with every passing moment.

Rebecca flings the curtain aside to keep an eye on it.

Jaime is agitated by these sounds. Don't let them get me, she pleads. Rebecca finds familiarity in this. Recollections of the helpless child she raised.

The knocks grow louder. Rebecca returns to the dark beneath her eyelids because it's the only way she can see her skittish daughter.

"You're hiding from . . . whatever's beyond the glass," Rebecca says. This revelation brings more tears. It's the first clear breath Rebecca's had since the murder. Validation that follows two long years where the scariest possibility at the time had been that she'd lost her mind.

Jaime has nothing to add and Rebecca can't allow that anymore.

"Answer me," she says. Through squeezed eyes, Rebecca slams her head against the bathroom tile. Has to reach for the soap tray to steady her balance as her thoughts turn inward to the influx of pain.

Her daughter resists.

"Jaime," Rebecca screams. Her head rams tile again, knocks Jaime loose this time. She's there in the dark, shrieking, because her mother has somehow found the void. Jaime's blank white eyes and distended mouth are an inhuman sight. Not the little girl Rebecca raised, not even the corpse she'd been forced to identify, but a mockery of her.

Rebecca jumps. The ceramic tub is slick with water and pinkish swirls of blood rushing from Rebecca's forehead. She stumbles into a net of mildewed shower plastic. It traps her, sends her spiraling into a cocoon that goes spinning across freezing linoleum.

Rebecca wiggles free and crawls for the carpet, her head cracked and bleeding. Eyelids heavy as she reaches tattered Berber and then keeps going. The air in here is different now. It's grease. Heavy grease that gets her stomach rumbling.

When the hell was the last time she ate?

Tacos.

Tacos while in the jail cell. That's what it smells like in here.

"Oh shit." Her words are mush. She uses the bed to get up on wobbly legs.

The door to her room rests just above the jamb, propped open on the lock bar. A greasy tray of takeout tacos sits on the corner of the bed. Directly across from the mirror. On the ground there's a crumpled sheriff's jacket. The old comforter in a pile beside it.

The glass stands silent. Sated. Even the bathroom hammering has ceased.

Rebecca reaches for her clothes, slides back into them.

She climbs onto the bed. It's safer there than on the floor. Closes her eyes and tries to square her thoughts. Jaime's gone again and for the first time Rebecca realizes why. The girl is using Rebecca's body and mind to hide from whatever's behind those goddamn mirrors.

The reason Rebecca knew to come to Bright Fork at all is because she fished it from Jaime's subconscious.

Rebecca looks at the mirrors like at last she understands. A humorless smile forms and feels good. She's getting somewhere and understanding is everything in her line of work.

Rebecca leaps the small chasm between beds. The tacos go bouncing, spilling beautiful grease and pork into the rug. Somehow, she's still thinking about the manager and how he's going to be enraged by that.

Her feet touch down on the floor. It's going to have to be a quick sprint to the door.

And don't look at the mirror, she thinks. Whatever the hell you do, do not look at it.

She makes a run for it.

Catches Jaime's reflection in her peripheral as Rebecca's wet hands clasp the knob, struggling for a grip.

The glass parts again like water, a stream of dark liquid comes flushing for Rebecca as she flings the door and rushes headlong into the night.

Her body slams against the second story deck rail. Her torso bends over it. The sheriff's squad car sits in the parking lot beneath, orphaned.

Rebecca whirls back around. In the split second remaining before the door clicks shut, in the collapsing space between the jamb and the door, one flickering eye widens with delight as it sees her.

Then it's gone. Or at least blocked off.

Rebecca goes running, shrieking, and panicking. Rushes to her car and dives behind the seat. She cannot get away fast enough. Fueled by urgency, she flicks the ignition and stomps the gas.

Speeds off remembering something else.

Cassie's house has a mirror problem, too.

22

The phone rings on her way out to the Pennington place. Rebecca's skin feels loose and the muscles beneath it are tight.

She's so desperate for familiarity, she figures Bret can fill that vacuum as good as anyone. Clicks the green answer button and puts the device to her ear.

"What the hell did you do?" Bret says. It's not a tone she wishes to hear.

"Bret–"

"The police were just here."

A deep, regretful sigh. "I'm sorry."

"Christ, there's no way back. Not from this."

"I know that. I'm so sorry."

"Why? Tell me why you did it."

". . . I had to."

"You're a murderer now, Becks. I mean . . . his parents?"

"They knew."

"Knew what?"

"What he did. And they had the gall to beg forgiveness on his behalf."

Bret sounds like he's hyperventilating. A crashing sound on the other end of the line–glass smashing across the floor. Nobody's ever wielded impotent rage quite like him. "How could you do this?"

"Someone needs to."

"God, you've really lost your fucking mind. You're nuts."

"Any port in a storm." Bret's father had used that saying when he was a child. Rebecca would get no points for throwing it back in his face tonight, of all nights, but the statement had never been truer. She had needed to kill Paul's parents, and the worst of it was how little it bothered her after it was done.

"Tell me what that means," Bret says. "Like, you'll kill anyone just as long as they're connected to him?"

"No," she says. She says that, but thinks, Maybe. "But they knew."

"The hell did they know?"

"He's killed three people here. That I know about. They knew he was fixing to do that. I think he might've killed more."

"What did they say to convince you of that? Specifically."

"It's what they didn't say."

"So you guessed. And for that, you killed them? That's why you had to escape? Kill the only chance the cops would ever have of finding the boy who–"

"It's been years. If they wanted to find him, they would've put some effort into it."

"This guy. He didn't just take Jaime from us. He took you, too. I lost everything because of him."

Then why aren't you out here moving heaven and earth to find him? Rebecca isn't going to ask that, though. She no longer respects Bret enough to bother. A better person might envy his tepid Christian sensibilities. But the truth is Rebecca just thinks him a weakling. Nothing admirable about turning the other cheek against those who punch for a living.

You've got to catch that fist and break every bone inside it. That's the only way to stop it from striking again. Men like Bret have made this terrible world. A world where evil is empowered to prey on children. Collectively, the world *tsks* its tongue while reading about tragedies over morning corn flakes, only to forget before the day's out. Distracted by bread and circus.

Emotion is naiveté. Better to kill that part of you before it bites like a dog.

Rebecca wants to say all of this. Instead she closes her eyes and feels the wind rushing through the cracked window. The only thing she does say, and at barely a whisper, is, "It's better like this. Believe me."

"The cops are on their way."

"I don't think they'll find me."

"Bright Fork? They already know where you are."

"I don't know where I am."

"Jesus, girl, you need help. Why won't you take it?"

"We tried it your way, remember?"

"You barely tried."

"I was forgetting the best things, not the worst ones."

"You didn't give it enough time."

"How dare you say that to me."

"Well–"

"No. I'm done. You don't know what I went through in there."

"They'll find you." The way he speaks, it sounds like he's hoping for it.

The highway sign hanging down off the overpass seems to be written in old relic and just looking at it makes Rebecca's eyes heavy. "We'll see."

"My God, you're never going to get out."

"It doesn't matter."

"It did to me, you know. Once upon a time . . . it really did."

"Not to me," Rebecca says. "Not since she died."

"I loved her, too. You know that, right?"

She ends the call and tosses the phone to the seat.

Pulls over to the side of the road and begs to see Jaime's bloody face once more as tears fill her eyes. She feels broken and alone and the only thing she needs is a little more time with her baby girl.

"Please," Rebecca says, voice wracked with sobs. "Honey . . . please."

Jaime's there. In the dark, begging her mother to cross over and hug her.

23

NOBODY ANSWERS THE DOOR.

For some reason, Rebecca stands and knocks like manners even matter any more. Her knuckles get tired of inquiring, but the knob refuses to give.

So it's a slow lap around the house.

The grass is up to her thighs all the way around the perimeter. She's thankful to be wearing pants for how many ticks are likely waiting to pounce off the ends of these bending blades. The house is pitch black inside and out.

She wonders if this place ever had electricity. Doesn't seem to be an electric meter on the property, and no power lines come anywhere close.

She feels sick as she spots the slumped scarecrow wobbling against the dwindling dark blue sky in the distance.

The windows here have been hastily blotted in the time since her last visit. Her fingers brush glass and return with a stain that's nearly dried.

She completes her pass around the house and finds a living

shadow on the porch. It stands inside the opened doorway. Beyond it is a house somehow darker than the sky.

"Know what's funny," Cassie says. "Knew who you were the second you showed up. I ain't talking 'bout now, either. I remember your car, sure, so I knew it was you coming back to see me tonight. But . . . the other day . . . when you showed up here? I knew who you were."

"Hi, Cassie." Rebecca rises from the tall grass, busted. For the first time, she can't think of anything else to say.

The young girl laughs on sight, her suspicions confirmed. "Already told you . . . you won't be the one." Her voice rises into a tantrum. "I won't let you."

"Oh, but that's not what he wants, is it?"

"I know what he wants," she screams. Her boisterous thumb stabs her breastplate in an assertion of superiority. "Better than him, I know."

Rebecca catches a glimpse of those empty eyes in the moon's glow and realizes what she's up against. Raging hormones hungry for the only boy her world has ever known.

Sometimes, older boys know this about younger girls. Some might say they use it to their advantage.

In Cassie's mind, this was never about anything except competition.

Cassie hops down into the grass and storms across the moonlit yard, shoulders rising and falling, psyched up to do something terrible. Or maybe already has. Her naked body wears thick splotches of crimson red, gore that fits like a suit. A stubby, hook-shaped skinning knife drips steadily into the earth.

Rebecca braces for contact, certain she cannot diffuse a blade attack in her current condition. She used to carry pepper spray on the job, more effective than a firearm and without the lasting responsibility of bullets. If things got bad, you could actually spray and pray. What she wouldn't give for that little canister clipped onto her keychain now. Because when it comes right down to it and you're squaring off against an armed maniac, you'd rather they pull a gun than a knife.

"Hoped you'd come back," Cassie says, high on the idea she's holding all the cards. "Questions you asked . . . way you looked at me . . . some dirty momma wanting to lick the blood from my ass?" Her head tilts back and she roars hysterically. Points the dripping blade outward so Rebecca doesn't get any ideas. Bitch is young and crazy. Doesn't mean she's stupid.

"What have you done, Cassie?"

The girl waves the knife at the door, orders Rebecca to get marching.

The two of them go, and Cassie shoves her along, steering clear of the parlor and the stairs, driving Rebecca instead toward the kitchen at the back of the house. The whole interior reeks of paint. Dark satin is brushed across each of the windows to keep the outside world way the hell out.

And as soon as Rebecca reaches the kitchen, she understands why.

The teenager drops into an old rusted patio chair and catches her lolling head on the inside of a blood-smeared palm. She rubs deep red streaks across her face like camouflage, realizes Rebecca has come no further than the jamb and kicks a seat out toward her.

"Stay a minute," she says.

Rebecca isn't interested in sitting. Isn't paying attention to the girl at all anymore because . . . what exactly has happened here?

"Hey," Cassie says, bringing the situation back into orbit. "I told you to sit. Break bread with me, bitch."

The 'bread' Cassie's looking to break sits on the table, beneath a copse of agitated flies. Here's a potluck of coiled innards and organs stewing inside a broken ceramic pot.

The smell hits like a punch in the gut, but the young girl doesn't seem to notice. She's too busy leaning over her plate of entrails, scooping a forkful into her mouth and scrunching her nose as she chews like a cow.

"What did you do?" Rebecca says.

Cassie's throat bulges. A couple of harsh swallows choke it all down. Sits back and rubs her belly with a fake, contented sigh. "Wish I had a toothpick. Stomach lining's the stringiest damn thing. Practically hides in your teeth."

"Cassie–"

"Swear, I'm gonna have meat sweats if I ever finish this."

Rebecca forces herself over to the chair but keeps it as far away from the table as she can. Buzzing flies continue to circle in excited patterns. The girl barely cares, seems delighted to have company–this particular company.

"I know you know about The First," Cassie says.

"I know something about them."

"Of course. You don't ask the questions you were asking unless you planned to go all the way."

"All the way where?"

The girl waves her off that track, uses her dripping fork like a pointer. "Here's something you don't know . . . something Paul said. Ima pass it along . . . guess that kinda makes me your history teacher." She giggles again. "Ever hear of . . . shit, what do you call them?" The girl stares off until her eyes become the size of golf balls. Slaps the table as the answer lands in her brain. "Totems! Totem animals."

"I think so," Rebecca says, afraid to agree or disagree. "Sacred animals, right?"

"Indians or whatever you wanna call them used to forbid the eating of totem animals . . . you know, the animal that represented their tribe. Kill a totem animal, and it's the same as killing and eating the village elder."

The spiel sounds rehearsed. Cassie pulls every word of Paul's lesson out of thin air.

"You know a lot," Rebecca says.

Cassie grins like the very thought of Paul is dreamy and then offers singsong praise. "He taught me everything."

Rebecca thinks, Of course that's what this is about. Paul could've just as easily talked her into joining the Peace Corps.

This thought makes Rebecca feel apocalyptically sour, and she realizes her passenger is stirring. Jaime wants something else, begins threading violent urges through Rebecca's head.

"Anyway," Cassie says, "you can't eat a sacred totem." Her fork picks at another slice of innards. "So, it becomes taboo. Like sucking your daddy's dick or whatever." She laughs uncontrollably hard at this. "If it's taboo, someone's gonna want to do it. Crave it. There's a penalty for it in those old tribes. Sometimes it's death. Doesn't even matter, though, because the thrill of the forbidden is what's driving you."

The girl takes another bite and chews with a gory smile.

"Some risk it . . . 'cause if you kill and eat the elder, you're climbing toward God on the skulls of your betters." Cassie pulls another cracked plate from a stack and drops it at Rebecca's station, spoons a glob of human innards onto it.

Rebecca feels nauseous, watching the warm blood pool evenly across the dish like melted butter. "I stopped for lunch on the way," she says.

Cassie waves a hand through the air. Forget it. "Paul told me never to do this," she says. "Always spoke about it like it was for other people. But he was wrong. He's the one who's leading us back, sure, but why should you and him get to have all the fun?"

"Leading us back where?" Rebecca says. Then realizes she doesn't need the answer. She knows where Paul's gone.

"Stop asking the wrong questions," Cassie says. "You need to eat, same as me. We all gotta eat before it's too late."

"Why eat?"

"Ask me again, bitch," Cassie hisses. "I told you he's gone and I meant it. Right now, the only responsibility he has is to come back. Everyone should be getting ready for that."

"The cars at the motel."

The girl nods and stuffs her mouth.

"Ready for what?"

The girl smacks her tongue. "Eat and find out."

Rebecca feels that rage rushing back. Jaime's in there building it like a campfire. She thinks about the way Paul fucked Cassie all over town. And how everybody knew it. Rebecca feels both betrayed and excited by this perversity, wishing she could've been at Herbert's barn to help cut Dalise Cortez out of her skin. And then she thinks she'll do anything to get these sick thoughts out of her head.

"What did you do to the sheriff's sister?" she says.

A fond smile spreads across Cassie's face. She slams her knife down on the table. "Ever skin a body? It's like tearing the flesh off a grapefruit."

"You killed her?"

"Paul didn't have the stomach for that part, so yeah. I had to do the killing. Killed all of them and he loved me for it. Loved me for doing all his heavy lifting. Hear that?"

"Who is everyone?"

"C'mon . . . Jaime. I thought you knew things."

Rebecca ignores the taunt. "Maybe I want to hear it from you."

Cassie clicks her tongue. "Sheriff's kid sister was nothing. Paul had eyes for her and I sorta did too. Killing her was just . . . well it was time to move on. Get serious."

"And the priest?"

"Yeah," she says. "Had to get him out of the way for—"

"Of course." Somehow, Rebecca already knows. She thinks about the priest at St. Cecilia's. How excited he'd been with the realization Rebecca could see both worlds. Jaime stirs at the thought, and that excitement betrays her as Rebecca fishes one errant truth from their shared mind.

That priest was Paul.

Even though it looked nothing like him, it was. He'd been waiting for Rebecca because he knows who Rebecca is.

Rebecca begins to stand. Cassie looks riled, but it's Jaime who diffuses her. Don't bother, Mom, she says. You won't find him there again. He was only there to help me find my way back.

"Tell me about the night nurse," Rebecca says. "The woman you killed."

"No," Cassie says. "I don't think you need to know about that one."

"She's the blood sacrifice," Rebecca tells her. "Prime the Barrens for rebirth . . . just like the first time. The elder who went out to greet Tanner Red."

"Planted this knife inside her neck, watched her eyes get all stupid wide. Kinda funny when you see it."

"Hilarious."

Cassie grins. "Take a bite now."

"Really, I'm fine."

"You think I want to eat this slop? That's not the point. Eat. Now."

Rebecca takes up the fork. Her stomach twists. Spears an organ that pops and hisses and spits juices at her. Jaime's inside wanting to eat it for some reason Rebecca cannot grasp. Jaime forces Rebecca to lick her lips like it's Italian sausage.

Cassie tries to stop herself from laughing, holds her stomach because the sight of Rebecca struggling is just too much. Then she falls forward and retches on the table, spewing vomit all over the plate of entrails.

Rebecca pushes back and stands.

"Shit," Cassie says. "Shit! Now I need to start all over."

It's clear now. Totem animals were devoured in order to absorb the strength and wisdom of elders once upon a time, and much is the purpose behind this. A primitive way to absorb the strength and energy of gift bringers.

"Where's your mother?" Rebecca asks.

The girl sits wiping her chin with a full roll of paper towels. Shrugs. Rebecca spots blood spatters on the linoleum down the hall, pooling in front of an opened bathroom door. She knows, but has to know. Walks down there and peers inside. An empty sack of skin hangs over the shower rod like a spent towel. Still wet. Still dripping.

"I thought you knew," Cassie calls. "We're eating the bitch." Another laugh.

Rebecca puts her nose in the fold of her elbow. This place stinks bad enough without adding vomit to its repertoire. "Fertility," Rebecca says.

"You know it," Cassie purrs.

"They make clinics for that," Rebecca says.

"My insides work just fine. This is about asking for His blessing. And if you're not going to eat . . ."

Rebecca walks back and eyes the bloody mound on the table, thinking about how much she wants to. She maybe even leans in to the food, one last play by Jaime to make it happen.

Cassie gets up, inches toward Rebecca with the blade dancing in her fist. "Funny thing about cutting into people . . . you find out pretty quick that it's a lot of fun."

"You don't have–"

"Paul used to talk about you," Cassie says. "Only girl he ever loved, and how sometimes you need to do things to the one you love that you don't care enough to do to anyone else."

Rebecca takes a few steps back as the worst monster rears inside the girl's eyes. Complete and total jealousy.

"I never saw him look at me the way he talked about you."

"I'm not her," Rebecca says.

"You got guts lying to me. Know what I used to make Paul do?"

Jaime can't hear this. She'll do anything not to hear this.

"I used to fuck myself up to my wrist while listening to Paul talk about how he murdered you. Got me wetter than melting snow."

Rebecca does a slow retreat into the creaking hall. Her hands raise in surrender, even though the madness in the young girl's eyes will not be placated by a white flag.

Cassie slashes the air between them. Drags her feet forward as the knife whooshes with disappointment. "Consumption of human fertility makes the consumer more fertile. It's simple fuckin' math. I need to be ready for–"

"Tanner Red?"

"His blessing," Cassie says. "His cock. Both? Maybe they're the same thing."

Rebecca rounds a corner on retreat and swings into the living room. Her fingers scratch the wall to keep herself oriented.

At her back, the clinking glass begins on cue.

"Only got one question left," Cassie growls. "If you don't answer, ima carve out your cunt and eat that first."

Tapping fingers crawling glass. Rebecca has summoned it like a genie.

It grows louder but Cassie's too crazy to be concerned. "Tell me how I get there," she screams.

She doesn't know the ritual, Jaime thinks. She's too stupid to know the ritual.

Cassie slashes at Rebecca. Her head slips back against the glass and dips into dark water. It's like being lowered into the sink at the salon for a shampoo only she feels the fleet of clawed hands rushing up out of dark space, eager to tear her skull open and savage her memories.

Cassie stomps her foot in tantrum. "Tell me how I—"

Cassie never finishes asking.

The glass bends outward, but never breaks. It's not even glass anymore. Rebecca sprints away from it as a mass of liquid rushes the room, flooding the Pennington house with thick waves of oily disease.

Cassie screams, lifts an arm to her face as a poisoned tidal wave sweeps her aside. The young girl is caught in a whirling current. Her flailing arms fight it, but it's impossible to stay afloat.

Rebecca crashes through the nearest satin window with a lowered shoulder. Does a header into the tall grass and scrambles upright. Retreats with her back to the night, watching the busted glass with disbelief as Cassie's screams turn to sporadic glugs. Inhuman hands, scaly and spindly, break the surface, slow drips of glossy tar falling off otherworldly flesh. These hands take Cassie's head and stuff it beneath the muck as the liquid continues rising up past the window, somehow never spilling through the broken glass.

Tar-dipped arms reach through the jagged space, fingers curling around the flaked siding. Fingernails clack on rotted wood with threatening patience.

Rebecca leaves, knowing the mirrors are never going to stop looking for what's inside her.

24

ONE MORE STOP.

One night, a few weeks ago, Marci Rooker was on her way home from an overnight shift at St. Gabriel's hospital when she got off I-95 to take the road affectionately known to locals as "the Fork Connector." This road bridges the town of Bright Fork with the outside world.

The Fork Connector is a lonely stretch of tarmac that runs twenty miles without a gas station, houses, or any real signs of civilization. Its most local comparison is the 34-mile Kancamagus Highway that connects two New Hampshire towns, Lincoln and Conway.

The Fork Connector, much like the Kancamagus Highway, warns motorists of its lacking fuel options as a way to mitigate potential bad luck. And depending on the time of night, it's not uncommon to go the entire drive without seeing another vehicle.

A sick mind might see it as the perfect place to stage a murder. No one's going to interrupt your business here. And if you're a victim, there's no place to run.

Marci Rooker had no place to run when she stopped that night, playing the role of Good Samaritan for two psychos posing as stranded motorists.

It's not hard to find the spot where she died. It's one little patch of anonymous land right off the pavement. It stands today as a roadside memorial.

Rebecca goosesteps wilted flowers, curled Polaroids, and an old teddy bear. There's a few splotches of darkened dirt that must be the girl's lifeblood. She bends and touches her fingers to it, feels a swell of rage.

The other vehicle sat right here on the edge of this gulley. Rebecca's boots hover halfway in empty air, because the earth falls abruptly away, spilling down into a barren countryside.

Cassie admitted to crouching by the tire, paring knife in her fist. As soon as Marci Rooker came to assist, Cassie sprung and stuck the knife through her throat, twisting the blade like a can opener and carving a hole the size of a Titleist.

"Monsters," Rebecca mumbles and wonders if she's including her daughter in that judgment.

If so, the voice inside her doesn't like it.

"What the hell's that?"

A string of torches light the evening in the far-off distance. You'd have to descend the gulley and cross the desolate field for a mile or more in order to reach them. Jaime wants to go down there, but there's something about the way those fires burn, black smoke and the scorch smell that wafts through her nostrils, even at this distance, that makes Rebecca resist.

Jaime flexes and Rebecca feels her body start to move. Involuntarily. A restless leg spasm. Rebecca knows it's anything but that. Before she can do anything, her daughter surges again and moves Rebecca forward, starting down the incline toward that distant torchlight.

"Don't," Rebecca says, sounding vulnerable and terrified. It's the tone of someone who's anything but in control. Whatever's out there, she just doesn't want to know. Feels instinctively that it would be the end of the line.

Jaime laughs, recognizing her power here. This whole time, she's been doing it wrong. Been trying to guide her mother's thoughts when, really, it's Mom's body that's easier to control. If only there was a fucking manual for this sort of thing.

"You used me," Rebecca says. "That's what Cassie knew."

Jaime laughs again, thinks, I had no choice. Thinks, You're not going to listen to that crazy thing, are you, Mom? Because she was crazy . . . something I very much am not.

And with that, the body starts toward the fires once more. Rebecca grabs the nearest branch in order to anchor herself, but Jaime fights that, too. She denies all resistance, forcing the fingers to open and close indecisively around the jutting limb.

Rebecca stares at the erratic motion of those dancing torches. The way they rise and fall, zigzagging to the rhythm of old music tucked away even further inside the distant night.

Jaime tries one last time to get the body moving, realizes Rebecca still has too much control.

"Stop doing this to me," Rebecca screams, her voice teetering on madness.

Her daughter thinks, I'll turn you inside out if I have to. I'm getting out in time.

Rebecca starts back for the road, but her muscles lock while gleeful and familiar laughter fills her head. Jaime was stuck with that laugh from an early age—always a mischievous baby, always hiding Mom's things and laughing uncontrollably as Rebecca would go around the house trying to find whatever was stolen. That cruel streak, revived in full.

You can't ever prepare for a day when your child turns against you. Rebecca feels nothing but misery. All the mourning, the life she traded, the relationships she torched and the people she slaughtered . . . everything in service of making this right. Vengeance built on a lie.

Everything. For nothing.

Rebecca's head is heavy. Two trains of thought barreling down very different tracks.

Jaime refuses to get back on her feet. Everything below Rebecca's torso feels like long-hardened cement. Rebecca sinks her claws into the earth and makes fists in the dirt in order to pull her body toward the road while tantrums fire off inside her skull like cannons.

You weren't supposed to figure it out, Jaime says. You're not supposed to stop me from seeing him. You won't! You can't!

Rebecca's fingernails crack and break on the asphalt, blood drops seeping through those jagged splits as she continues to pull. Inching across concrete like a wounded animal. If she can just reach her car, she'll leave Bright Fork behind . . .

No! You won't do that!

Rebecca thinks she'll turn herself in and keep this terrible monster imprisoned inside her skull forever.

Oh, you're going to let me out. Right now.

Rebecca's close. Her blood-slicked hands reach up, stretching every last inch in order to clasp the handle. Jaime relents, sensing if she pushes the body too far against Mom's will, then the bones will snap like a twig. She returns just enough control for Rebecca to get to her knees and hurl herself into the driver's seat.

Twists the ignition and stares out at the fires one last time.

It's not too late, Jaime thinks.

"Yes," Rebecca says. "It is."

This is what I want, Mom.

Jaime sounds like a little girl again, the way she used to ask for presents on Christmas.

"God, Jaime." Rebecca's tears come on hard. "You're a monster." Her lungs are heavy and from the inside of her head, her daughter continues her battle for control, steering her off, not toward home, but back to Bright Fork.

25

EVERY SPOT IN THE MOTEL IS filled. Rebecca has to park in the space that reads "Office Only."

Jaime may have receded into the background, but she isn't prepared to let her mother leave here without retrieving that book.

In and out, Mom . . . just like that.

Rebecca treks up the stairs to her room and uses her key to twist the knob, pushes in. It gets caught on the chain.

Graceless bodies fumble through the dark. A bed sheet rises like a ghost. "Who's there? Is it time?"

Rebecca checks the plastic key to make sure the number corresponds. "You're in my room."

"Take it up with the front desk." Pudgy fingers curl around the door's edge to hold it in place. The face stays beneath the dark, save for a pudgy chin with fly hair scruff.

"Where are my things?" Rebecca says.

"Take it up with the front desk."

Rebecca throws her shoulder into the door. The squatter makes a surprised sound and pushes back, startled by her ferocity. All she needs is to break that goddamn chain and then she's going to break his fucking nose.

"Help me, will ya?" the squatter screams. Another shuffling body joins in the back and forth and the sheer weight of the intruders wins out, stuffing the door back into its jamb.

"What are you doing in my fucking room?" Rebecca screams, but the conversation's over.

This place is stuffed full of guests. Even Paul's old room is seemingly occupied. A flush of light surrounds the drawn curtain there, and a bunch of silhouettes are beyond it. Rebecca presses a curious ear to the door and hears nothing.

She goes down to the manager's office to let him know she's been evicted and he's nowhere to be found.

Instead, a man she's never seen before stands behind the desk. His posture's straighter than an arrow and detached eyes glare off into space. His joker's grin is oddly permanent. Rebecca crosses his line of sight and his eyes flick over to her while his expression remains unmoved.

"Hello?" she says.

No response, but those eyes continue to stare.

Rebecca spots her duffel bag on the storage rack across the room. She takes it without any protest, finds nothing missing. The book sits right atop a wrinkled ball of clothes. She's evicted because Bright Fork is suddenly the hottest destination in the state. Rebecca fishes her last handful of Advil, mined from the bottom of her pocket, and steals a bottle of soda from management's mini refrigerator. Remembers the days when she used to worry about ingesting all this aspartame and dealing with the cancerous fallout.

At least her mom had the luxury of dying like an everyday person.

Rebecca checks her phone on the walk to the car. Part of her wants to go home more than anything else, but she realizes she no longer remembers what she'd be going back to. Flashes of that life exist in her mind, but it's about as real as living someone else's memories.

Rebecca sits behind the wheel, staring numbly at the orphaned Sheriff's car parked where Cortez had left it. Then she remembers

Paul's face and knows she'll never have another day's rest if she quits now. Gets lost inside the death wish daydreams that carried her this far.

"You're welcome to stay with us." Three people surround the rear of her car, spaced out like they're posed for an album cover. Two women are hidden in the shadows of overhanging trees and a man stands closer. He's young, early thirties, carries a look that says he was birthed in billions. Clean-cropped hair, rimmed glasses, a tailored suit that probably cost as much as Rebecca's apartment. "Small town," he says. "Limited places to stay."

"I'm okay," Rebecca tells him.

"Why? 'Cause we're strangers?"

"Sure."

"Ollie," he says. "There. We're not strangers anymore." His feet scrape gravel as he moves closer, leans in. "Come on. Stay with us."

The girls giggle. Rebecca feels self-conscious around them.

Ollie reaches through the opened door. His fingers are manicured, cut with precision right down to the quick. "We're all wondering, you know? And if this really is the night . . . well, we just think maybe it's healthier for you to wonder in the company of others. Right, ladies?"

The ladies don't bother to answer. They pass a few muted whispers back and forth, sprinkling in mean girl giggles so Rebecca doesn't get any ideas about becoming part of their clique.

"Do you really believe in this?" Rebecca asks, vulnerable in the moment and hoping the answer's no.

Ollie's hand recoils a bit. How could a true devotee ask such a skeptical question? "What do you mean?"

"Tanner Red," she says. "I want it to be real."

Now he smiles like everyone here's getting away with something. "I know what you mean," he says. "He's been nothing but whispers, just a pile of rumors for so long. Hard to believe we're on the verge of finding out."

"I'm scared, you know?" Jaime's insecurities come tripping past Rebecca's lips. "Like, what if it's all for nothing?"

Ollie flashes a philanthropic smile. "Why don't we learn

together?"

Rebecca closes her eyes and mumbles, "Yes."

Ollie opens the door like a chauffeur and ushers her out. The girls follow behind them, moving together through the darkened parking lot to their room at the end of the first floor.

The girls giggle again and Rebecca feels their eyes on her back, judging her age and her clothes. Her demeanor. Everything. She wonders how she's supposed to blend in to this. Can't ask many questions because she's supposed to be on the same page.

I'm on the same page, Jaime says. You don't have to worry about it.

Ollie opens the door to his room and everyone piles in.

Rebecca spots the mirror against the wall before he can flick the lights. The glass seems to wink in headlight glare from passing traffic. Jaime goes into panic overdrive, seizing Rebecca's movements. Jaime tears the comforter off the bed and drapes it over the mirror without looking at it.

"What are you doing?" Ollie laughs.

Jaime doesn't answer. Too busy taking care of business. She pulls Rebecca's coat off her shoulders and storms the bathroom, hanging it up over the mirror to blunt the knocks that have already resumed.

"Listen to me," she says. "Do not uncover these."

"Hard to look at yourself sometimes, right?" Ollie says. The girls give 'ain't that the truth' nods. Then it's just the four of them standing in fragile quiet listening to the taunt of muted knocks.

"Looks like we picked the right person to offer our companionship," Ollie says. He points at the glass. "That's a sign."

Rebecca points too. "That's not what you think."

"I don't know what to think," Ollie says. "But I hear there's evidence of the crossing in this very motel."

"There is," Rebecca confirms.

Ollie's eyes turn the size of quarters. He takes her hands in his. "What did you say?"

"There are signs." Rebecca points to the ceiling. "In a room just upstairs. They're allowing small groups of people in to see it."

"Someone has given their body to Tanner Red." Ollie smiles. He goes to the mirror and the bedspread covering it starts to rise. "Is this . . . Him?"

Jaime laughs at his ignorance.

Everyone looks to Rebecca as the adult in the room. For the first time, the younger girls care about what she has to say. Rebecca realizes now that she recognizes at least one of them, and maybe both. Singers? Actresses? Never one to be star struck, she can't care enough to ask, but their fashion and jewelry suggest money, though Rebecca stopped paying attention to that stuff decades ago.

The brunette clears her throat and lines the desk with trails of coke from a little vial nestled between her breasts. Oh, Rebecca thinks. Definitely Hollywood. The brunette slides her dress off at the shoulders and it shimmies down her legs without a hint of modesty.

The four of them chase away the lines. Rebecca's nose tingles at the burst of alertness even as her nostrils go numb. She's never used before, but it turns out Jaime's no stranger. Rebecca is too far beyond betrayals at this point, can't help but wince at this. She always figured her kid would be one of the good ones.

The blond girl begins to undress as she sniffles. "Shit," she says, catching a few blood patters as they drip from her nose. The brunette caresses the blond's body anyway, licking the little driblets off her small breasts with a gentle giggle. Both women reach out for Rebecca to join them.

"No thanks," Rebecca declines.

They couldn't care less about being rejected, kissing and groping without a drop of curiosity for the tapping mirrors.

"It starts with the flesh," Ollie says, brushing fingers over the naked bodies. "A display . . . for Him."

"A tribute to His generosity," Rebecca adds with Jaime's knowledge.

Ollie has a trace of disbelief in his smile and Rebecca thinks it's because, to him, this whole thing is probably this month's trendy religious cult.

Rebecca slumps into the chair and positions away from the action, wondering if she's this desperate for company. Realizes that Jaime's been keeping her here. The amorous noises grow loud enough to draw Jaime's curiosity. Ollie is naked now, sliding into the brunette and thrusting without any rhythm or emotion. Her natural breasts sway in hypnotic circles while she eats the stick-skinny blond squatting over her mouth.

Ollie glistens, instantaneously sweaty and pumping behind an expression of forced concentration. The girls groan like bored porn stars, both of them looking like they'd rather be anywhere else. Every thrust is obligatory, each moan, perfunctory.

Ollie says, "Come here" while continuing to push deeper inside the brunette. The blond never looks up at all. Just buries her face against her forearm, writhing along because that's how this has to start.

Rebecca shakes off his invitation, but Jamie isn't so repulsed. She leans into the action, watching the bodies spend themselves. They're right, she thinks. They need to show Him.

"Please," the brunette cries. She watches Rebecca with an expression of beautiful agony no different than the mugging faces she's made in a dozen music videos. Her stretched and wiggling fingers beg for companionship.

Rebecca remembers her now. Ten years ago, they'd gone to see her in concert for Jaime's birthday.

Rebecca continues to refuse, though both mother and daughter are witnesses to the show.

Ollie seems tired. Almost pained. He reaches out for her, too, his eyes begging for mercy. As if Rebecca can stop any of this.

Though maybe she can.

That means finding Paul.

If this is real and it is happening then there's only one way to do that.

No guarantees, Mom, Jaime tells her.

There never are.

26

REBECCA RUSHES TO THE SHERIFF'S car. The doors are locked and Cortez's keys may no longer be in this world.

"Okay," she mumbles and goes back to the manager's office. The smiling man is still there. Still smiling. His head remains motionless, though his eyes are active, following her wherever she moves.

There's nothing of use in here. Rebecca slams her palms on the counter, ready to force some answers, when the sight of this stoic freak up close brings second thoughts. His eyes bulge, and while his mouth ticks up in a frozen smile, there are no age lines on his face. His skin is smooth, coated with a careful application of foundation. Whatever the hell's underneath that, she doesn't want to know.

She inches past him to the manager's small personal space out back. The smiling man never turns, though Rebecca half expects to see his eyes peeking at her from the back of his head.

The manager is back here. Wedged all the way against the far wall, mounted atop a swivel chair his killer was able to roll out of sight. He's the color of chalk and an axe juts from his chest. Every drop of blood that lived inside him has relocated to the floor.

Rebecca crosses the small space like she's moving through rain puddles. Closes her fingers around the hilt and rips the axe free like she's been chosen to wield Excalibur. Something about the weight of the blade in her hands is satisfying, makes her flush with power.

She almost hopes the freak show in the next room will try and stop her on the way out.

I want to kill him, she thinks.

But nope. His back's to her as she leaves. Once she's through the front door, Rebecca steals one last look and finds only his eyes are watching her go.

Cries of ecstasy are muted in the parking lot. Thumping furniture combines to make a strange and deliberate rhythm. Those muffled sounds are the only noises haunting otherwise silent air. Seems as though each room is invested in proving their willingness to Him.

That thought brings goose bumps to Jaime's arms.

"Stop it," Rebecca growls, but her daughter only laughs.

Rebecca marches to her car, drops the axe across her lap and cranks the ignition. It stutters but never starts. She tries again. Jaime's laughter fills her head, thinking, Wow, this is some really bad luck, Mom.

Rebecca doesn't believe in luck. The stench inside the car is terrible. She flicks the cab light and turns toward the backseat. A scarecrow lies slumped against the window. The burlap sack has no eyes, looking instead like an executed hostage in an ISIS video.

The body is sheathed inside a lace gown. Fabric split down the center, leaning far enough to one side to reveal the hay-stuffed stomach cavity.

"The innards," Rebecca says as she steps back out into the lot. Cassie was eating her mother's innards. The scarecrows on the outskirts of town had lost theirs, too. It's part of the ritual.

Jaime plays dumber than a dog. Pretends not to understand what Rebecca's talking about. Even that's a tip off because Jaime says I don't know and then keeps repeating it.

Rebecca isn't biting. She lifts the axe and rushes across the parking lot, hammering the Sheriff's car window and cracking the glass into a thousand pieces. "You think this is going to scare me off?"

The axe head clears away the rest of the jagged pieces as motel guests begin opening their doors, whispering to one another. Nobody seems to know what to make of this.

The town of Bright Fork is so desperate to stop Rebecca. And yet nobody's made a move against her.

Rebecca circles Cortez's car, chopping the side mirrors clear. Does her best Dukes of Hazzard to get inside. Tears the rearview mirror free and hurls it into the parking lot. Uses the axe head to chop through the steering column and pull a handful of wires free so she can hotwire this thing to life.

She hits the flashing lights. The hotel guests lift their forearms to their faces in perfect unison.

They're waiting for the sign, Jaime says.

"Let them wait."

But I want to speak to them. Jaime tries wrestling control of the body. She uses enough force to make Rebecca feel as if she's suddenly outside herself, watching helplessly even as it's Rebecca who reaches down for the shifter.

"What did I just say?" Rebecca screams in the tone of a scolding parent.

Jaime recognizes the emptiness of the threat, laughs.

"Okay," Rebecca says. "When I find Paul, I'm going to chop him to pieces." She smacks the axe head with the back of her hand. She builds images of Paul's splattered and broken corpse. Vivid enough for Jaime to relinquish all control, stunned by her mother's ferocity. Because Jaime never thought her mom would try and kill him out of spite.

Right, you little bitch, Rebecca thinks. It's not a threat. I'm killing him if it's the last thing I do.

Rebecca hits the road.

27

REBECCA LAYS IT ON THE table on the way back to the Fork Connector.

"You know you ruined me, right?"

Jaime greets that with cavernous silence.

"Yeah," Rebecca says, taking grim pleasure in the truth. "You know, and you don't care." The logical extension of motherhood Rebecca always knew was coming. No matter what you do, it's going to be a thankless end. "Did you ever care?" she asks aloud, adding, "About anyone other than yourself?"

I care about Paul.

"What have you ever done but take things from me?" Rebecca demands.

I love him, Jaime says.

"You used to take twenty dollar bills out of dad's wallet when he wasn't looking, as if we didn't know. You were in grade school. We dealt with that, knowing you were going out for burgers and shakes at the bowling alley."

Yeah, I'm a monster.

"Remember how you used to shoplift . . . even things you didn't need? Or want? And when you got caught, I bailed you out and convinced the store to avoid pressing charges. Only to have you turn around and do it again the very next day? And when I told you that you were going to have to accept responsibility for your actions, you told me I should die."

I was a teenager. Awful, right, Mom?

"Maybe you are." This is cathartic. The sudden freedom to condemn an ungrateful child. "I tried giving you space," Rebecca snarls. "Tried debating your worst ideas in order to show I was interested in you. None of it mattered. You never cared about me at all."

That's a lie, Jaime says. Doesn't bother to elaborate.

Marci Rooker's roadside memorial is up ahead. Rebecca cuts the wheel and skids across the entire street. She leaves the car there with flashing cherries to throw pulsing blue and red lights on the tree line. Make the motel followers think the jig's up if they ever figure out to come here.

So now you want to go out there? Jesus, Mom, make up your mind.

"I'll go," Rebecca says. "If it'll end this." She steps to the edge of the road and spots those dancing torches still burning. A beacon lighting the way.

The trees standing on either side of the thin trail somehow sway heavily in dead air. The hillside slope descends forever. Muck swallows Rebecca's shoes with the sound of a plunger. The flat field seems like it's just another foot or two away, but she's always descending toward it, never reaching it.

I, uh, think we need to go back, Jaime says.

Rebecca weighs that suggestion, decides Jaime isn't interested in her mom's well-being. The girl's scared. Actually scared of what Rebecca's fixing to do. "Oh, I don't think so," Rebecca growls.

What do you think you're going to see out there?

"You tried very hard to get me down here just a few hours ago."

Jaime thinks, Shit, then catches herself–remembers she's on the same circuit as old Mom. These wires every kind of crossed.

It's not that I wanted to go out there, Jaime tells her. It's that I'm finally learning how to control you. I thought I needed to climb my way out . . . literally. And you know how close I almost came? But it turns out that's not it. I only need to settle in. Become you.

"Lock me away inside my own body," Rebecca whispers. "Not going to happen." They both trudge willingly toward the torchlight. Rebecca lifts the axe as if to solidify her determination.

Finally, she stomps down onto flat earth.

The moon occupies the entire sky like an exaggerated matte painting in an old sci-fi movie. It lights the way and bathes the world in a ghost-white glow. Everything's ethereal.

Rebecca glances back. Curiosity and perhaps one final vestige of reluctance. Jaime does her best to exploit this, begs to go home. The hill Rebecca has just traveled is no longer there. Nothing is. Only the lonely expanse of darkness.

"We're the veil," Rebecca says, plucking that from Jaime's brain.

Jaime only laughs. A cutesy giggle filtered through adult lungs. Rebecca used to find that sound adorable in her little girl.

The ground is softer here, squishier, and the air is squalid. The stench of a locker room at halftime, complete with the stink of two-dozen spent bodies.

Jaime thinks it's beautiful, forces Rebecca to weep at the sight.

"What happened to you?" Rebecca says.

Nothing. This response is immediate. Adamant. We worship the flesh. Flesh inspires Him. Therefore, flesh brings good fortune.

"You had a loving family," Rebecca says. "We did our best with you."

Don't be a greedy gopher, Mom. Not everything's about you.

Rebecca can't take the irony of that thought. It busts her gut and makes her keel over. Real, bona fide laughter, because it's the only thing you can do when it's all for shit. There are a million responses she can offer but holds her tongue. Jaime glances at a few of them as they move through Rebecca's brain and says, Wow, you don't think too much of me.

To cite these perverse beliefs as some kind of hope fills Rebecca with despair. It's nothing more than a horrible practice held over from a primitive world. And yet there are people in that motel so eager to belong to it. Who wish to touch a God who'll touch back.

Jaime begins to fight Rebecca's legs, making them feel like jelly. Suddenly, she'll do anything to prevent her mother from reaching those torches.

"What are you afraid of?"

You, she says. You're crazy and I'm not going to let you kill him. I thought I could control you. But you're fighting me so . . . damn . . . hard . . .

The ring of fire nears. Circling and dancing flames scratch the onyx sky. Old stone steps scale to a rounded platform floating high over black oblivion.

Each step dips beneath her weight, but Rebecca's quick. The torchlight is oddly welcoming, licking her face with warmth as she nears. Her footsteps echo like horse clops and deep down inside her, Jamie flails in panic.

You can't!

"Can't wh–"

Rebecca sees him. At last. The man she's thought about for two years straight. The one who ruined it all.

Paul.

He kneels in stasis. Positioned in a way devoid of physics, looking more like a still frame from a movie. His body leans at a harsh angle, arms stretched overhead, reaching for something long passed in the sky. His naked body wears dark-streaked splatter and the way his face is twisted reveals a particular madness about him.

Paul is anything but lucid. His features are sunken, nearly decayed. Impossible to believe this is the healthy twenty-two-year-old man Rebecca once considered her future son-in-law. Skin's pulled tight over his skeleton, but the sharpest edges of bone are in danger of tearing through. Every bit of muscle has been sapped away. His eyes are open, soft brown orbs floating in piss-yellow pools.

There's nothing left in this man. He's given everything away.

It makes Jaime's heart beam. Mom's too late. The only thing she can think is, He made it. He actually made it through.

Rebecca, on the other hand, feels nothing. No satisfaction. No anger. Certainly no relief. Paul has taken himself out of this world, denying her the one reason to live this long.

She feels sick and foolish over the things she's done to get here.

Visiting Paul's parents.

The memory of a falling hammer as it smashes through a skull, mashing the brain beneath. The way that body goes limp, save for its horrible and twitching face.

Or the gun barrel pressed so hard against a forehead it leaves a ringed depression as watery eyes plead and realize it's hopeless.

It's what she came to do.

And you think *I'm* a monster.

"You are," Rebecca growls.

Jaime grows defensive. Hers was not a sacrifice made lightly. Paul hadn't wanted it at all. But Jaime had to be the one to cross, don't you understand? She couldn't let another woman go on ahead in her place. No way, given what Paul was planning.

"Why did you let me think he killed you?"

Jaime laughs. It's a wicked sound Rebecca's never heard.

You had to get me here, Mom. Nobody else could've done that.

Rebecca is a transporter. That was her role. She looks down on the rotted face frozen before them. Paul seems to grin.

Rebecca lifts the axe, thinks, Fuck all of you, and drops it. Paul's head shatters like a frozen pumpkin.

Jamie screams so hard the noise comes out of Rebecca's mouth. Rebecca puts the blade to her own throat next, ready to yank the hilt.

It's the only thing left.

But, oh, Jaime's been expecting this. She flings her arm outward and, with a bend of her elbow, casts the weapon into the night. It never lands, never rattles across the ground below. It's just gone.

Paul remains frozen in place, a thick sheet of red pus pumps like a geyser from that headless spigot.

Rebecca thinks, finally Bret was right, but it's too late. Rebecca is almost gone, sapped of the will to continue. Revenge is the battery that had kept her juiced. But it's dying, bringing Jaime into control. Her thoughts dominate this brain as the body learns to dance more steadily to her daughter's music.

"It'll take some getting used to," Jaime says. "But you're in pretty good shape." She settles behind Rebecca's eyes like the driver's seat of a used car. The body's odd—older, achier, groaning knees, imperfect vision, and a twitch at the base of the spine. Wear and tear that comes with age, Jaime thinks and smiles. Yeah, I can make this work.

Rebecca is stunned by just how little she can fight it. It's a gift in some ways, because she thinks she's been dead since that night two years ago, and all of this was some vision of hell glimpsed between the single blink of an eye.

When you're called into the morgue to identify the body of your baby girl, the pall is so dark it can never really lift. And that worsens in the days leading up to the funeral, as you begin making arrangements. Choosing the dress the body will wear, the photo for the casket, the eulogy you've got to somehow write . . .

How can you talk about nineteen years of life? That's the snap of a finger.

Then there's the burial, the last goodbyes. Ain't a parent on earth who wouldn't swap places with their child to give them another chance. To avoid the despair you feel while standing on that cemetery grass, shivering in that always-autumn chill, no matter the time of year.

And yet, Rebecca feels nothing but hatred for her daughter.

"I wish it was different," Jaime says. She turns away from Paul's splattered remains. The field has returned. Maybe for Jaime it was always there.

Paul's body is long gone, too. Even the bloodstains are missing atop the stone tile, the last remnants of a waking dream.

Jaime's awake now.

"Time to see Him," she says. "I've waited long enough."

Rebecca's last thought before she slips away is, Yeah . . . let's see Him.

After everything, she's at least curious.

She's never met a god before.

28

WHY PAUL?

I'll tell you why Paul.

I mean . . . he was never much of a worker. We know that. But . . . what a dreamer. I loved his promises.

He never got bit by that stupid 9-to-5 bug, knew there were other ways to make a living. Only education he wanted was the one life teaches.

He wasn't dumb or lazy . . . just different. Always thinking about the way life really works. Remember when he and I both got accepted to UMass? I don't think I ever told you just how quickly he dropped out. It was after one walk through the bookstore, tallying the amount he was going to have to pony up for a single semester's worth of books.

"That system," he said. "That system's gonna squeeze every dime out of you, honey. Books you won't read, classes you don't need. Parking fees, meal plans, an adviser who thinks you're a number, who will push you to take four classes a semester knowing full well you can't graduate in four years that way. It's to their benefit they keep you here longer. And the really stupid ones will get pushed into other majors and then be left stranded on the job market without sellable skills. Higher learning's a meat market."

Some might disagree, but hey, he sold me.

I remember going home that day thinking maybe it isn't for me either and Dad jumped down my throat, saying I wasn't going to ring groceries the rest of my life.

I went to class while Paul took a job at the Fairview Country Club. The pay was under the table, north of nothing special. He trimmed flowerbeds, whacked down the weed crops that grew in knots around hole ten, and learned how to set the John Deere's mower low enough to the ground to keep the fairway clean.

It wasn't glamorous work, and Paul knew that. It was an act for the money people. A way to prove to them he knew the value of an honest day in the field.

I wasn't surprised to hear Paul had ingratiated himself to others. Even you'll agree, Mom, that his confident smile can turn your heart to butterflies. Make you think there's no one better.

Because there isn't.

The country club loved when he worked charity events, caddying for VIPs who were amused by his gift of gab. They helped him to build connections with local businessmen and state-level politicians—all part of his plan to claw his way to the next strata.

Paul took weekend work, too, pool cleaning and landscaping. Whatever those VIPs needed. He came home one day and told me how he got lured into a million-dollar kitchen when the bored housewife of some international CEO caught herself a doozy of a computer virus.

The wife, all bronzed wrinkles, peeled three one hundred-dollar bills from her wallet and slapped them on the counter—his, if he could fix it right now, no questions.

He could. And did. That would've been that, if not for one accidental glance at her browsing history just before clearing it away. One URL out of the ordinary, the only thing that wasn't social media and gilded specialty shops. Something he'd never heard of before and couldn't access—FindingTheVeil

It was something we weren't supposed to see.

The site was behind a firewall, accessible only by password. A password he wanted. So Paul sent Old Miss Bronzer a phishing email that injected custom JavaScript into her browser, grabbing all the usernames and passwords off it.

Dick picks, compromising videos of hubby and underage mistresses—incriminating stuff, but not the Veil.

What was the Veil?

Well, we didn't know. And it turns out nobody really did. Hence this website. FindingTheVeil. A digital secret society. A community of one-percenters from every corner of the world, each dedicated to solving the mystery by pooling evidence found in their personal collections.

What mystery?

Well, it's all sourced from one single page. A page that's older than time, they say. An illustration of a girl in coitus, her face crudely ecstatic and thrown back, upside down, so she's at the bottom of the page. Her legs shooting up in a V. Between them a dangling curtain.

A veil.

From that website, Paul gets the names of other members.

Names whose laptops he eventually breaks into with the same JavaScript key.

He finds more digital whispers there inside the bodies of encrypted emails, digs them out from behind password-protected folders, and swipes the most careless sketches and document scans off unsecured clouds.

Paul abandons his goal of ladder climbing, quits his jobs and goes off the grid. Because this veil is the only thing that matters.

What's behind it?

We get drips of information that wouldn't fill a bucket.

It becomes an obsession.

The document that pointed the way for us was Arabian. Paul found it sitting on the hard drive of an actual Saudi prince. The scan of a page that's locked up tight somewhere inside the Kingdom. It was sent encrypted to London for translation and the discovery yields a name never shared with the rest of the Veil Community.

It's not exact, but the words were close enough to resemble Tanner Red. Maybe it's like a game of telephone where the meaning changes the further it gets passed around, and maybe He doesn't care what we actually call Him so long as He's worshipped.

The deeper we get into this world, the older the documents become. Scans of yellowed pages, scrawls in a written a language no one's ever seen. Yeah, you've seen it, Mom, but let me tell you . . . very few people on this earth have.

The language is alive. It slides the worlds around like . . . I dunno, some kind of Rubik's cube, opening doors and then closing them just as harshly. Why do you think the book can hide in plain sight? Why nobody else recognizes it for what it really is?

Anyway, we begin putting these pages together. What few translations exist. It takes every hour of every day. Soon, we know what we've got.

The oldest secret.

A world of rituals and trespasses. Efforts to resurrect these practices inside temples hidden from both Christian and Islamic faiths.

We're no historians, you know? But how is it possible for civilizations on two separate continents to worship the same ancient deity? Then I remember some random nugget from school, real diamond in the rough bit of info. How at some point long ago the world was once a single continent. I start to wonder how old this Tanner Red really is.

What's funny is that the members of FindingTheVeil could've found all of this themselves, except they couldn't even trust their own secret society in full, keeping things hidden from the rest because everyone among them wanted to be the one to finally figure out how to cross over and bring Him back.

You snooze you lose, right? It's Paul who becomes the first to understand this history in full. Tanner Red in the New World and the women who killed a god. There's mention of a book taken from one corner of the world to another. Pages that describe these events in full, and many things far older, brought to the New World and hidden inside the Village of Gar.

Unlike all the empty faith and mysticism in this world, here's a god who'll show His followers the secrets of the universe. All they need to do is be faithful . . . and ask.

We start to resent the powerful people and their efforts to conceal this secret. Like everything else, they want it for themselves.

But now, Paul's got it. A roadmap.

And most importantly, nobody knows it.

Nobody except me, and I'm sorry to tell you this, Mom, but it's so much more interesting and fulfilling than any part of the world you tried to prepare me for.

What nobody knows is there's a way back for the vanquished god. He'll come through a ritual, after a willing sacrifice has surrendered her body and can still prove loyal. This is meant to signal the complete and utter rejection of lesser faiths. Denial in the concept of an afterlife, not because there isn't one, but because we have no interest in going there. His religion is flesh. Flesh is so much more interesting.

Do you know what it's like to discover that? Like, parents are always making the mistake of telling their kids they can be anything they want to be. We can't, and that's a bitter fucking pill to swallow, you know? But for me? Well, when you find out that you can become the bride of a god and all you've got to do is find the balls to check out of here . . . well, that shakes you up.

And at first, it's a bad feeling. Like coming to the end of a treasure hunt and realizing that not only did you forget your shovel, but you can never get one.

That's how Paul reacts. Sulks around the apartment feeling like it's over because self-sacrifice is a bridge too far—or is it?

I wondered that while going to class, pretending to think about anything other than that possibility. There's nothing like taking a few political philosophy electives to push you over the edge. You listen to college kids drone on and on with regurgitated talking points like they're the first fucking idiots to ever have these thoughts. And this while the professor pretends to be dealing with free thinkers and grown ups? It's so depressing.

My mind's made up. And now it's my turn to get Paul to come all the way around.

You wouldn't believe it, Mom, just how little he wanted to kill me.

What scares him worse is what he needs to do after I'm gone.

It's monstrous. Because he needs to actually reach into that void and give himself over to Tanner Red. Be the one who's going to carry Him back. If he's gonna send me on ahead, then he's gonna be right behind me . . .

I don't think either of us really wanted to walk anything back. We were scared, yeah, who wouldn't be? I watched you come home every day, Mom, dreading the next morning, tired of talking about your day. We both saw the boredom in your eyes. It sucks. There's just nothing in this world. It's slavery. And if my life is my own, then I'm going to use it any way I want.

Paul didn't think he could do it.

Not at first. I stripped, got him going with the hardest fuck he ever got. Have to fuck for Tanner Red because that's what gets His . . . blood flowing, I guess. Ha ha. Power comes from bodies, you see, and we've got to imprint so our spirits can follow each other to the next life where our bodies will be different. Because they're going to be.

We drove to the woods, never exchanging so much as a word the entire way out there. I guess our minds had diverged as reality set in. Too late for either of us. Curiosity is about to make Paul into the world's most reluctant murderer. There's no turning back now.

I got on my knees, flipped my blond hair behind my shoulders while flashing the most confident half-smirk I could manage. Holy shit, my heart was beating so hard I thought it was going to explode, but I was also high off the action because I knew, just knew, this was real.

"Get slicing, baby," I told him. I really sold it, 'cause it's easy to sell. "Now I know what it feels like to go to space." But it's even more impressive than that. People have gone to space. Nobody's ever come back from the dead.

It remained to be seen if I would, but I wanted it bad enough to try.

Paul wasn't some goony boy when it came to the opposite sex. Always got on well with listening. Just listen, and don't deny a woman once you find out what they want. That's the rule. He takes it to heart. I've been telling him what I want for months. He holds the glinting blade to my face, twists his wrist around, momentarily entranced by all the different ways the light glides off steel.

And I can tell by the look on his face he's having second thoughts. My fingers fall gentle on his knuckles. A smile breezes past my mouth. Too nervous to keep it there, but as long as he gets the assurance he needs.

"Give it," I say. "Go on and—"

He makes a sound on the roof of his mouth like sprinklers chinking. Tears begin to nest, and I only have a second to notice them. Because then he starts sawing through my face like it's a restaurant steak. Peels the strip all the way down to my chin and tears it off with a snap. The gushing blood's incredible. Feels like . . . a mud mask. I'm too numb and too cold to feel any serious pain, but to watch my blood squirt him in the face like a water gun?

Well, it's always surprising when you find something so weird you can't help but laugh. That's right, I laughed as I was being murdered.

That knife curves and slices wider. Cold steel moves beneath my face. It digs under my skin.

The worst of the pain is my eyes. One strip of flesh peels up across the round of my forehead and traces down along the edge of my jaw. My teeth chatter like a freezing skeleton. Cherry red tears, Mom.

The only thing I've got left is the nodding assurance in the eyes of the man I love. And I swear, it's like he can read my mind because he's nodding up a storm. And weeping, and before too long, even tells me how much he loves me.

Paul cups the back of my head with his free hand. Hovers close, nose to bloody nose and says, "I love you so much." Kisses my face. Exposed nerves explode like a handful of firecrackers.

But I don't care. That's not what this is about.

There's too much blood loss. My shoulders loosen and pull me back to the floor. The world is going weightless. Eyes heavy.

"Do it," I tell him with mush in my throat.

"Oh, I'm going to." His knees are on either side of me. He speaks in pointed tongue, words that aren't his. He always did study those secrets with more scrutiny.

The blade slips in between my ribs and pierces my heart as he chants. It's like dying in fast-forward. They always say time slows down as you're on your way out. But that's a lie. Everything speeds up.

"I love you," he says, trying to snuff out a demented laugh.

"See you there," I tell him and slip away. The last laugh is with me. I'm already going.

My last thought, just before my body dies, is of you, Mom.

Hoping you're gonna be comfortable.

And I gotta say, you are.

29

JAIME PULLS THE RINGING PHONE from Mom's pocket, sees it's Dad calling.

"Hi," she says in Rebecca's voice. It's difficult to not call him Daddy.

"Becks," Dad says.

Jaime thinks for a second the signal's lost because there's a long pull of silence that's only getting longer. Then she hears a half dozen little intakes of breath, realizes he's become a sputtering mess.

"This isn't the best time," she says.

"You've made that real clear."

"Oh, don't be too hard on . . . on me."

"Listen," Dad says. "I'm at the end."

"I know. Everything is."

"The truth is this, all those times you needed me to keep your head straight . . . wanted my help to put you right . . . I needed you just as much. I'd wake up every morning waiting for that phone to ring, desperate for your voice."

"That's . . ." Jaime doesn't know what to say. She knows she should feel guilt over this. For the way she dropped her parents' lives into a blender. But what's coming is too great to care. She's so stymied she clears her throat and says, "We need each other."

Dad sighs. A scraping laugh that sounds more like incredulity. "That's why I pushed you so hard to stay . . . I mean, the hospital . . . I'm sorry I forced your hand. Only wanted you to get better. For us. For me. Shit, mostly for me."

"I love you." That part's true enough, doesn't matter who's responsible for saying it.

"I love you. But now that you've . . . there's no way we can go back to the way it was. I'm all alone."

"Paul's dead," she says.

"Oh god." Dad can't get another word out. Tears have washed everything away. There's just sniffles.

"Relax, I didn't kill him."

". . . That's . . ."

"I think what you're looking for is 'That's good news,'" she says.

". . . That's . . ."

From this distance, Jaime sees the road. The flashing blue and red treetops where Mom's stolen car blocks the Fork Connector.

A string of vehicles are beyond it, each one sloped ever slightly inside the dirt gulley running parallel to the pavement. People have begun to pour down the hillside in a steady drip of unsure footing and awkward, mutual assistance.

On the phone, Dad has been talking. Jaime needs to tune him back in. If there was more time and less tension, she'd have summoned Mom back from the void and let her say a few final words to her dawdling husband. But the amassing bodies say to Jaime that it's happening, and soon. Her heart flutters with that realization. Dad's already an afterthought.

"So . . . you're coming home." For the first time since the funeral, he's got a tinge of hope in his voice. It's painful to hear. This was never about hurting them, though Jaime supposes parents should bleed for their children. And she knows Mom agrees with that . . .

"I don't think so," she says.

"Why?"

"You know I can't."

". . . Yeah."

Jaime pauses and searches the moonlight for inspiration. There's no magic bullet here. The pain she's heaped upon the Daniels Family has already done its damage. She just closes her eyes and mutters, "Live, Dad." Realizes with horror what she's said.

"Wait, what?"

She pulls the clothes from her body as she starts toward the gathering at the base of the hill. She lets the cool spring air breeze her like a sail, moving in a leisurely zigzag.

"I love you." She kills the call and flings the phone into the tall grass.

30

REBECCA FEELS TRAPPED ON A theme park ride. She glides on rails across the moonstruck field. The distance seems more manageable on the walk back.

It's silly to worry about modesty, though Rebecca can't help but think about how awkward she must look as Jaime strips her. By the time she reaches the others, she can barely stop her teeth from chattering.

A tent sits at the hill's base. The farmer's girl, Danielle, stands beneath it, presiding over rows of homemade pies and unloading stacks of paper bowls at the far corner. She watches Rebecca's approach with spring-loaded apprehension.

It's Jaime who diffuses the tension. "It's okay," she says. Points a finger at the crowd and flicks her wrist around. "This here's all for me."

The farmer's girl cocks an eyebrow and then her head drops to one side. "You're . . ."

"The Veil," Jaime says.

Danielle leans in on the table and smiles, gives Rebecca a slow once-over. Around them, other women begin to disrobe. Rebecca is ashamed to find relief. Lots of older, less shapely bodies help offset her insecurities.

The men keep their distance, pushing torch sconces into the earth and spacing them evenly all the way down to the far tree line–hundreds of feet away.

"Okay, ladies," Danielle says. She drops a plastic Solo cup on the table stuffed with plastic utensils. "Spoons up . . . dinner time." She uses the pastry cutter to slice every homemade pie into evenly divided pieces. The hearty aroma wafts up through the broken crusts before soupy red goulash rises through the cracks.

Jaime makes sure they're first in line, takes the largest portion.

Hell no, Rebecca thinks. She does everything she can to drop the bowl into the grass. Jaime chides her for the wasted gesture. "Come off it," she says. "We've got enough food for ten rituals." Jaime reaches for another bowl, tightens her fingers around it and concentrates on keeping them in place. "You drop this one, I'll just eat another. I'll eat this right out of the grass if I gotta."

Jaime takes a big bite, and Rebecca's mouth fills with warm hunks of white meat. Every bite is succulent, juicy, and mixed in alongside fresh potatoes and carrots. It's not bad. And the next bite is almost pleasurable. Cassie had just thrown innards into a dish like a savage, so desperate to belong without ever understanding why. But this . . . it's doable.

"You're doing good, Mom," Jaime says without a trace of sarcasm. Her tone is nurturing. Rebecca finds a dozen memories where she'd given her little girl similar treatment.

It's Rebecca's turn to plead. Anything to stop this. But Jaime's too eager and determined. She does all of this with a sense of pride Rebecca's never felt. You really believe in this, she thinks.

"I do."

Jaime wolfs the pie and takes a second helping. The other women are busy complimenting Danielle while exchanging muted whispers about what to expect from tonight. Everyone looks to Jaime like she's in charge. But she's not in charge.

She's a bundle of nerves. Jaime is about to see Paul again. Two long years imprisoned inside someone else's head, hiding at first, marinating in the unnecessary grief. Pleasantly surprised to discover just how much her mother loves her.

It is the only way.

And yet, Rebecca thinks, you've never even said you're sorry.

"Of course I am," Jaime snaps. The others look at her and take skittish steps back. Jaime puts the empty plate on the counter where the farmer's girl takes it away. Jaime is already moving out of earshot. "You think I wanted this?" she says. "I had no choice in the body I take. Needs to be blood."

Fine, Rebecca thinks. But tell me why. You owe me that much.

"Why?" Jaime whispers. "It's real. That's why. I think of all those mind-numbing masses you and Dad used to drag me to . . . you know, on the holidays when you pretended to be Catholics or whatever. And all the talk about faith and feelings, some higher power that's beyond us. Too good to touch our lives on the reg. Because, why? To be rewarded later. Maybe?"

So just be an atheist, Rebecca thinks. What the fuck do I care? You're grinding this axe because of Christmas Eve?

"You're not listening. They expelled Him on this spot hundreds of years ago. And I'm about to bring Him back." She cannot stop herself from smiling as she speaks. Pride overfilleth. "I'm about to wake up the world."

They've moved so far out of earshot they're standing roadside.

Rebecca thinks, You really do love him, don't you?

"You can feel that?"

. . . I can.

"That's good. That's the truth. And just . . . once He parts the Veil, He will be whole again. Think of the fortunes He will give to us, the devoted."

You knew I needed to carry you out here, Rebecca says. And the closer we got, the more strength you found.

"Be proud you solved it."

Didn't solve anything, Rebecca says. This whole awful case collapsed down around me.

One of the cars up ahead has its door ajar. It's the only chance

Rebecca has and she's been moving toward it. Now, she seizes it. She's able to wrestle control away from Jaime just long enough to throw herself into the seat.

Jaime realizes what's happening, uses Mom's lungs to scream for help.

In the distance, rushing bodies start toward them.

Rebecca doesn't need that long.

Just a second . . .

It's a struggle to reach the mirror. Rebecca's trembling hand reaches up, and Jaime fights for control of every finger–some of them wiggling while others remain part of a gnarled claw.

Rebecca reaches it and turns the mirror down just as Jaime flings her arm back against the seat, keeping it pinned against the cushion.

It doesn't matter.

"Take us," Rebecca screams while every last muscle goes into lockdown. Her eyes swing up to the thin slice of rearview glass, already turning into a pool of midnight ripples.

A tri-pronged hand with nails the size of railroad spikes reaches from the side mirror, thick tar running off its forearm as it stretches into this world.

Now it's Jaime screaming for help. She's too close to give up now.

Somewhere in the night is the sound of footsteps on pavement.

A second hand reaches from the opposite side mirror. In the rearview, yellow eyes appear in the rippling water, reaching the glass and bending the frame outward.

The commotion arrives in the form of panicked party guests. They tear open the doors and drag Jaime to the pavement, even as the gnarled fingers swipe at them. The claw locks onto the closest guest, yanking him back against the side mirror. He goes screaming, his body folding, bending, breaking all at once, sucked through the tiny square hunk of glass at the speed of a vacuum.

Jaime goes rolling across the tarmac as the panicked people drag her away from the mirrors, several screams erupting around the car. Disorder she can no longer see.

They're dragging her back down the hill and Rebecca has no more strength with which to fight.

"Now I'm pissed," Jaime growls. "But that's fine. 'Cause what's coming next is all that matters and I can't wait to get you out of my head."

31

NIGHTGOWNS BILLOW THROUGH THE AIR in the distance like a bunch of erratic ghosts. The grass at her feet is tamped into patches of brown weeds. And the earth grows darker as she stomps over it, steps becoming charred crunches as the ground blackens.

The world's dead. Graveyard gray as far as the eye can see. There's only those fluttering sheets of loose fabric.

She shambles on, following in a dream.

A flute haunts the distant night. Who's playing it? Is anyone? It reaches her ears in short bursts of random tone and fuzzy air.

Then the virginal gowns fling into the sky like graduation caps. The wind catches them and sends them spiraling high over the countryside.

The liberated bodies find rhythm in the random notes, bending in spastic motions to accommodate them.

She stumbles toward the blackened hilltop, behind the other naked bodies, racing now for that ring of circular stone dildos. Each of them enthusiastic to embrace The Plowing Fields.

Twelve women.

Twelve phalluses.

Spread legs. Squatting torsos. Sculpted heads slip inside each of them, one at a time, as if this has been choreographed. Insatiable moans pass from their mouths, flying around the entire ring like an orgasmic echo.

She pauses in the center. The other women turn to watch. Their heads swivel in a slow, circular motion. They reach for her, desperate for affection she cannot give. She watches them grind away on the cold, unmoved organs and finds their undulation as painful as it is arousing.

The flute falls silent because now it's the constant bursts of elation that are going to summon Him.

The stone slab is cold. She sits on it, leans back on freezing hands. It's not at all the way she imagined it.

It's better.

The women get themselves off, stretching themselves wide in order to prepare. Their faces flash with fleeting jealousy. She's so turned on by it she barely feels the night chill.

The field slopes to one side and she spots a figure moving toward them in the far-flung distance. Misshapen, with shoulders burdened by weight she cannot see.

She feels strange and uncomfortable watching it approach and the way it moves fills her with the kind of dread she's never felt.

Because whatever that is, it isn't human.

The surrounding moans reach crescendo and begin to drop off. Detonating orgasms turn the group over to exhausted silence, leaving crumpled bodies gasping for air as they prepare to witness the arrival.

The figure moves along the planted torchlight, following it all the way from another world. The women–all shapes, ages, and sizes–shriek as if they're watching a rock star take the stage.

The shape changes as it nears. It sheds shadows and emerges in human form, coming with a familiar gait. Somebody she's seen. A slim torso hardened by muscle.

She begins to weep.

Reaches out.

Spreads her legs wide.

He steps to her.

It's about to work.

His lips lean in and find hers. He grins and she loops an arm around his neck in order to hold him in place. Just wants to look at him.

Remember him . . .

There's the little appendix scar that runs from his belly to his ribs, but even that's faded and almost non-existent now.

He runs one hand over the smoothness of her belly, prowling up to her small breast and giving it an unfamiliar squeeze. Unlike her, he has nothing to remember. Jaime's body is all bones, long buried.

Paul isn't exactly Paul, either. He smiles and the torchlight finally gives her a full view. It's Rebecca's mind, nearly extinguished, that catches this. Here's the priest from St. Cecilia's.

I could've killed you there, she thinks.

"No," Paul says. "You couldn't have."

His hands are like winter stone and his touch chills her spine.

In the moon's glow his flesh takes on that same translucence from the church. And there's an inhuman shape moving beneath it, gliding back and forth like a parasite hiding inside a host.

Jaime reaches out and takes him in the palm of her hand. The simple touch makes him purr. "I'm ready," she says and then braces for it.

Rebecca retreats further into her subconscious.

Jaime wraps her legs around Paul and digs her nails into his back, cracking his skin and peeling it away like hunks of ice, her hands finding the flaky paper of a hornet's nest beneath. Behold, the flesh of a god.

Rebecca can't fight this. She feels the love Jaime has for . . . it. It's more than she's got left. Every parent worth their salt wants this very thing for their child. The one thing that's almost certain to elude them the rest of their lives.

Happiness.

And, Jesus, Jaime's got it in spades.

Jaime bucks as He pushes deeper inside her. The voice is still

Rebecca's, but Jaime wields it. Moaning and screaming His name now, not Paul's, because it's been so long and it feels so good and there was never anyone else.

"I love you so much," she cries.

Her enthusiasm ignites Him. Inspires Him. His rhythm twists and she's already close.

Rebecca's thoughts and memories are on the precipice, and she casts them willingly into the void, one-by-one. This peace she feels is new.

Here's the choice. And it isn't much of one. She thinks of that night with the macaroni lion and holds that memory in her hand when all the others have since jumped into the abyss. At last she has an answer to the question of what that night represents. Jaime's future. She's grateful for it. And then Rebecca hurls it too into oblivion with the rest of her mind.

Jaime throws her hands on His shoulders, desperately trying to keep Him close as His flesh continues flaking off under her touch, revealing that gray-skinned, featureless hive creature beneath. Its coiled and dangling mouth falls to her breasts, sucking greedily on them. His flickering tongue is a swollen insect with its own dancing apparatuses. It tickles her flesh, bringing indescribable pleasure.

The crowd gasps. Begins to chant excitedly.

Jaime should be terrified, but Rebecca searches her thoughts and finds nothing of the sort. Even now, there's only love.

And Tanner Red handles her with the same amount of care. Every thrust fills her with warmth. Fills her with hope. Fills her with the truth.

This whole time, Jaime was right. Paul was right.

The book was true. They did what the members of FindingTheVeil could not. Many of whom are probably here tonight, basking in failure.

That matters. They deserve this. This puts Rebecca at ease.

Rebecca was certain it was revenge she needed. But now her little girl's come back.

It's not worth fighting anymore. With one final bit of energy and like a dying star, Rebecca sends one last beam of light and love to her daughter.

Gonna tell our baby all about you, Mom. What you did for us.

Rebecca thinks that's nice. Something to remember her by.

Overhead, dawn starts to break. Warmth beating down the frost. At last, spring is in the air.

ACKNOWLEDGEMENTS

This book wouldn't have been possible without the following contributions and support.

Thanks to Carrie and Andy at Grindhouse for giving this book a home, and for making sure it got done right. You guys are the gold standard by which all other small presses should be judged. I mean that sincerely and I'll work with you again in a heartbeat if you'll have me.

Scott Cole, for somehow knowing what should go on the cover of this book, and then for designing it. And much love to the rest of the Black T-Shirt gang for their continued advice and support: Adam Cesare, Pat Lacey, Aaron Dries.

Special shout outs to Gabino Iglesias for supporting his fellow authors like it's a full-time job. J. David Osborne for insight and wisdom when I needed it. Erik Van Der Wolf and Buz Wallick for that special thing we're working on.

Last, but not least, my endlessly supportive wife, Michelle, who gets to deal with having a writer in the family. I'd include my kids, too, but after reading this book I'm not sure it's a great idea to remind you I have them.

- Matt 3/30/19

ABOUT THE AUTHOR

Matt Serafini is the author of *Ocean Grave, Island Red, Under the Blade,* and *Feral.* He also co-authored a collection of short stories with Adam Cesare called *All-Night Terror.*

He has written extensively on the subjects of film and literature for numerous websites including Dread Central and Shock Till You Drop. His nonfiction has appeared in *Fangoria* and *HorrorHound* magazines. He spends a significant portion of his free time tracking down obscure slasher films, and hopes one day to parlay that knowledge into a definitive history book on the subject.

His novels are available in ebook and paperback from Amazon, Barnes & Noble, and all other fine retailers.

Matt lives in Massachusetts with his wife and children.

Please visit https://mattserafini.com/ to learn more.

Other Grindhouse Press Titles

#666_*Satanic Summer* by Andersen Prunty
#049_*Saint Sadist* by Lucas Mangum
#048_*Neon Dies at Dawn* by Andersen Prunty
#047_*Halloween Fiend* by C.V. Hunt
#046_*Limbs: A Love Story* by Tim Meyer
#045_*As Seen On T.V.* by John Wayne Comunale
#044_*Where Stars Won't Shine* by Patrick Lacey
#043_*Kinfolk* by Matt Kurtz
#042_*Kill For Satan!* by Bryan Smith
#041_*Dead Stripper Storage* by Bryan Smith
#040_*Triple Axe* by Scott Cole
#039_*Scummer* by John Wayne Comunale
#038_*Cockblock* by C.V. Hunt
#037_*Irrationalia* by Andersen Prunty
#036_*Full Brutal* by Kristopher Triana
#035_*Office Mutant* by Pete Risley
#034_*Death Pacts and Left-Hand Paths* by John Wayne Comunale
#033_*Home Is Where the Horror Is* by C.V. Hunt
#032_*This Town Needs A Monster* by Andersen Prunty
#031_*The Fetishists* by A.S. Coomer
#030_*Ritualistic Human Sacrifice* by C.V. Hunt
#029_*The Atrocity Vendor* by Nick Cato
#028_*Burn Down the House and Everyone In It* by Zachary T. Owen
#027_*Misery and Death and Everything Depressing* by C.V. Hunt
#026_*Naked Friends* by Justin Grimbol
#025_*Ghost Chant* by Gina Ranalli

#024_*Hearers of the Constant Hum* by William Pauley III
#023_*Hell's Waiting Room* by C.V. Hunt
#022_*Creep House: Horror Stories* by Andersen Prunty
#021_*Other People's Shit* by C.V. Hunt
#020_*The Party Lords* by Justin Grimbol
#019_*Sociopaths In Love* by Andersen Prunty
#018_*The Last Porno Theater* by Nick Cato
#017_*Zombieville* by C.V. Hunt
#016_*Samurai Vs. Robo-Dick* by Steve Lowe
#015_*The Warm Glow of Happy Homes* by Andersen Prunty
#014_*How To Kill Yourself* by C.V. Hunt
#013_*Bury the Children in the Yard: Horror Stories* by Andersen Prunty
#012_*Return to Devil Town (Vampires in Devil Town Book Three)* by Wayne Hixon
#011_*Pray You Die Alone: Horror Stories* by Andersen Prunty
#010_*King of the Perverts* by Steve Lowe
#009_*Sunruined: Horror Stories* by Andersen Prunty
#008_*Bright Black Moon (Vampires in Devil Town Book Two)* by Wayne Hixon
#007_*Hi I'm a Social Disease: Horror Stories* by Andersen Prunty
#006_*A Life On Fire* by Chris Bowsman
#005_*The Sorrow King* by Andersen Prunty
#004_*The Brothers Crunk* by William Pauley III
#003_*The Horribles* by Nathaniel Lambert
#002_*Vampires in Devil Town* by Wayne Hixon
#001_*House of Fallen Trees* by Gina Ranalli
#000_*Morning is Dead* by Andersen Prunty